day 1

"R, let's go to big beach, 5 days of party, is going me, MV, D, L and the girls" said G

so G is this half man with a nice built, kinda buff you know but ripped with nice abs, the kinda of guy that works out alot, and this group of guys normally is well accompanied if you know what a mean, you may be thinking i'm saying this girls are prostitutes and shit but they are not, i swear they just really good looking girls

so R is like "hmmmm, i don't know"

but then G said something that really got R

"stop with that gay shit"

so R was like

"okay"

so R packed his things, G passed by R's house 1 hour later, he was driving the car wearing a sunglass. it wasn't a nice sunglass, it was too big and he is a small dude so he kinda looked like a chiuaua. on his right in the front sit was MV. he is a big dude, smaller than R though, but bigger than G, but he got nice shoulders. i don't know what kinda of shoulder workout he is on but it is some nice shit, he probably does arnold press. on the back sit where 3 girls, on the left was JV which is MV little sister. she is a tight bodied petite girl with nice formed titties and a nice ass. on the middle was silicone titted asian A, which got this model like body, like tall and skinny with long legs and the silicone addition was a nice touch, she got that on point like a lot. i think she putted like 250ml, and that really fitted her body. on the right, behind MV was silicone titted M, she is a petite black haired girl with a nice fat ass and a huge silicone, personally i don't think she putted the right amount silicone, she putted 500ml which i think it was too much for her but no one is complaining, plus it looks nice on pictures. so when G pulled up, she could have sitted on silicone titted asian A's lap, but she got out of the car so R could get in, and when R got in the car she climbed on R's lap. she is sexy as hell i'm not gonna lie, and R could feel her booty buns closing on his dick but R didn't get hard. with everyone settled in G started our way to the marina, where we would get the boat and sail to Big Beach

"who's playing today?" said silicone titted asian A

G looking straight ahead, answered

"today is a house concept party, no big names but a nice party"

"i can't wait for the 30th" said JV

"VC is so sexy" said silicone titted M while she adjusted her position on R's lap

"his sets are really good too by the way" said MV

"i don't care about his sets, i just want see his mulatto face with that indian headdress" said silicone titted M

"just don't sneeze on your panties when you see him, because we won't go home to change " said JV

so with all this sneezing on the panties shit, R tried to calmate the situation

"who's in the marina already?" said R

so G answered

"D, L and the girls are already there"

so silicone titted M said

"what about B, isn't he going too?"

"i said D, L and the girls, hihihihi" said G

"you are poisonous G" said siliconed titted asian A

"i can't believe he got out of the closet. JV, your mom is close to his, did she say anything about that?" said silicone titted M

"HAHAHAHAHA" laughed MV

then he said

"my dad told me his father hired prostitutes to fuck him straight, but the little butterfly just told the pros to stick a finger up his ass"

"i don't believe that" said silicone titted M

"i do" said R

"i don't want to believe that too, but that's what i heard" said JV "enough with finger up ass shit, MV did you hear who's going to be there?" said the little man G

"who?" said MV

"little S" said G

"nice" said MV

then he said

"did you see her new silicone, really majestic stuff"

"i gotta concur with that" said G

"magical like mickey" said R

"why don't you say that about my titties MV, they are majestic stuff too" said silicone titted asian A

i'm trying to keep the story straight and it doesn't make sense to me too but i guarantee you that this happened "they are nice too" said MV

"do you wanna touch them?" said silicone titted asian A

"no" said MV

somebody stuck a finger up his ass and he liked, R thought at that instance. but what R said was,

"who did them?"

"dr. fabian, he's an artist isn't him" said silicone titted asian A

i'm still trying to find words to describe what dr.fabian is till this day. as this talk got to a closure we were about to get to the marina. as G parked the car we could see the people that were already there

there was L, good height, long hair, good looking guy. and there next to him was D, a tall guy with short hair and a nice beard, he isn't good looking like that but he has a nice beard. on D left was B talking to C, M, J, BP and GB. B is a skinny tall dude, if he was a man he would be able to pull up a lot of girls if they didn't see his huge forehead. C was okay, brown hair, nice face, with a nice ass and nice titties, M on the other way was really sexy, nice tight ass, really big ass too and a really pretty face. J the same, nice body, huge ass, really good looking, but she needs a nose job asap. BP is sexy, 70% dark chocolate with a nice ass and really nice titties and GB is good looking, she is L's older sister, which makes him a lucky guy because she has a lot of good looking friends. as everyone got out of the car i gotta confess R's dick was half hard, it wasn't rock hard but it had some blood on it. the girls went upfront and G and MV waited for a second

"aren't you coming R?" said MV

"give me a second" said R while he tried to shake his dick soft it didn't work, his dick got harder, he didn't know what to do, he couldn't pull up in front of everyone with a hard dick

"that little devil, she did it on purpose" said R to himself

R got out of the car so G could lock it and R pretended to take a phone call

"hello" R said outloud

R placed the phone on his shoulder and said

"G, MV go ahead, its mom, i'll catch up in a second"

they went on through the marina gates through the wooden passage that lead to the boat , when little r, that of little has nothing was finally soft, R went through the gates of the marina to find everyone, but R couldn't find them

"they probably on the boat already" said R to himself

but the thing was, R didn't know where the boat was, so R called G, G gave R the instructions to find the boat and when R finally found them, everyone was already inside with cups on their hand. the girls had those g in cups, the big round ones, they are pretty nice, the guys had beers on their hands

R layed his bag inside the boat with all the other bags, grabbed a beer and went meet everyone. B and some of the girls were in the lower deck, R thought of staying there but when R heard how the conversation was going, something about a Roberto being B soul mate, R decided that the way to go was to go the upper level. there R found G, MV and L. D was no where to be found probably shitting or taking a phone call. some of the girls where upstairs too, silicone titted M and silicone titted asian A where there, JV, J and BP where there too

"i don't understand man that like man, imagine prefering a cock rather pussy, a hairy dude rather than a delicate faced woman. lo ok at this, look at this titties" said L while pointing to silicone titted M's breasts

"now look at my titties" he said while raising his shirt, he had hairy nipples

"why would someone. actually not why, but how does someone prefer man titties than girl titties, i don't understand" he concluded

.

"i don't know, some people prefer cocks in their face than being suffocated by titties " said MV

"would you suck a cock for one million dollars?" said JV

"bitch, don't even get me started, you chase dick to suck" responded MV

"so? i like to suck dick, but would you?" continued JV

"1 million dollars?" said MV

but before he could continue all the guys said

"bro, bro, bro"

"no, no, no" he responded

"hmmm" said JV

"i would suck your dick for free, if you want" said silicone titted asian A to MV

"not right now, not right now" responded MV

"guys is the story of the prostitutes fingering B ass true?" said L

"so what my dad told me was that he told his mom because he could not not hide from her anymore, he wanted for her to love him the way he was and not by a fabled construct that they imagine him being, and he asked her to not tell his father but she went and told his dad anyway and then his dad hired some prostitutes to fuck him like it was some kind of medicine of the flue or somethin g like that, but when he got to the house and opened the door to his room the prostitute was fingering his asshole" said MV

"his dad should have tied him with handcuffed faced up in bed and injected viagra in his vein" said L

"the prostitutes would have made him cum like a cow giving milk" he concluded

"i don't know about cumming but his dick would be raw meat when the prostitutes where done " said G

"it is indeed hard to cum on viagra" said R

"not that, i mean that too, but what i meant is that gay people probably don't cum with women" said G

"that's so mean" said BP looking at R

"i swear cumming on viagra is really hard" said R

"not that stupid" said BP

"yeah, that they don't cum with women" said G

"hiring prostitutes you stupids" she responded

"yeah, but you gotta see the other side too, no father wishes their son to be gay, every father wants to have little grand children, but if they are they are, but i do understand his side, he was emotional, acting out of impulse" said G

then, suddenly the sailor comes up to the upper deck and says

"G, the girl with the brown hair attacked me and took my hat, now she is topless in the front of the boat, its risky because she could fall off the boat"

we looked to the front of the boat to see her titties, it was C, she was tipsy tipsy d runk, and yes she could indeed fall off the boat

"i'll go talk to her" said G to the sailorman

as G and the sailorman walked down the stairs, D was coming up. he sitted next to silicone titted M and BP, he then turns to silicone titted M and says

"B told me your tits are fake, i think they are real, but the only way to know is by touching them"

"noooo, you're ugly, you can only look, no touching" she said

"i think he is kinda charming with that beard" said BP

"i don't mean he is ugly like ugly, he is ugly for asking to touch my babies" said silicone titted M

but right at that moment L says,

"look, look, look, look at G and C"

when we turn our head again toward the front of the boat G is kissing topless C with both his hands on her ass, as we turned our head back L said

"i think i even saw a squeeze in her booty"

"G is a really naughty boy, i wish he was naughty with me" said BP

"i can be naughty with you" said L

she gave a shy smile and turned her face to MV. as all of this happened G was returning from his ventures with the tipsy C

"damn she had a nice booty" he said

"you quick as hell man, you should be in formula 1" said D

"no, no, no, i just put her to bed, but i squeezed her booty to get a feel of it, nice as hell" said G

"i knew i saw you squeezing her booty" said L

"BP said you should be naughty with her G" said J

"did you really BP?" said G

"i didn't" said BP

"she did!!!" said J

"okay, i did!" said BP

"so are we gonna get naughty?" said G

"we will" said BP

as we finished our drinks the sailorman got up to the upper deck to tell us that we were arriving at the restaurant, we were going to stop at this restaurant to have lunch an d then follow to Big Beach. as the boat came to a halt, we were getting our way down to the lower deck. we descended the boat and landed on the middle of the restaurant, the restaurant attendant arrived finally

"table for 15" said G

"follow me" said the attendant

we all sitted down and ordered some drinks, the guys switched their beers for gin and tonics and the girls switched their gin and tonics for moscow mules

"honestly, i'll have a moscow mule too" said R

"it's so good, you are gonna like it" said silicone titted M

"hey B, is it true you had some prostitutes fuck you with a plastic dick" said D

"it wasn't like that" said B

"so how is it like" said D

"so my asshole father heard i was gay and he decided that i needed some vagina to 'cure' my disease, so im home alone chilling watching some tv when suddenly the door bell rings. i go to the door, look at the magic eye, and see this two woman. so i open the door when suddenly one started grabbing my dick while the other started taking her clothes off. so i tried to make sense of the situation and they told me they were hired to fuck me straight, so i told one to jerk me off while the other sticked a finger up my ass, better make use of the situation i thought to myself" said B

"really well thought" said D

"why did you asked her to jerk you off? arent you gay?" asked silicone titted M

"i mean, i still got a dick, hahahaha!!!" said B

"but how do you get it hard" said silicone titted M

"that's why the other one was with a finger up my ass, i imagine Roberto fucking me" said B

"B, B, tell them about Roberto" said tipsy C

"Roberto is my soul mate, me and him are going to get married and we are going to adopt some black children, Roberto wants 2, but i want 3, i want one vietnamese too" said B

"i want to vietmegetoutofhere with all of this gay talk" whispered L to G

"where did you meet Roberto?" asked silicone titted asian A

"i met him at halloween, i was dressed as a vampire and he was dressed as a hot dog so i told him that i really liked hot dogs and he said which kind of hot dogs i liked, so i said the one between his legs so he fucke d my ass real good so i couldn't walk straight for 2 days straight" said B

"Roberto sounds like a real charmer" said JV

"he really is" said B

"didn't you start to date too GB?" said G

"i did, just don't tell Cristopher" said GB

"who's Cristopher?" said G

"the guy i fucked yesterday, hihihihi!" said GB

"we won't tell Cristopher GB" said B

"but can he fuck me too?" he continued

"i don't know if he likes dudes but i could ask, maybe you could fuck him while he fucks me, who knows" said GB as GB said that, 3 guys showed up at the table and this average height, tanned with broad shoulders and nice pectoral muscles said directed to silicone titted M

"we are having a party at our boat, maybe you and the girls could join us after lunch"

"thanks for the invite, but we are with our boyfriends here, do you wanna go sweety?" silicone titted M said looking at G

but before G could answer, the guy said

"i was thinking of the ones that are single"

but silicone titted asian A said

"we all date here"

but then the guy said

"i doubt that, there are way more women here than man"

so silicone titted M said

"yeah, but he dates me and her, and he dates her and her and he dates her and her, and this one dates her, and that one dates her, but B is available"

"who is B?" said the guy

"him!" said silicone titted M pointing at B

"oh" said the guy and after that he left.

"didn't you think he was pretty" said silicone titted M to silicone titted asian A

"he was, but the guys here are better looking" she said while looking to MV

"yeah, i thought the blonde one was kinda cute, but we have to go to Big Beach anyway, you had really nice wits there, how did you do that?" responded silicone titted M

"i concur with that" said R looking at her wits

"i don't know, it just came to me" said silicone titted asian A

"this octopus looks good" said D looking at the menu

"that's because you haven't seen this octopussy" said BP

"yeah, but i like salmon sashimi pussy, you probably have tuna sashimi" responded D

"oh, sushi, i love sushi, do they have sushi here" said JV

"i'm pretty sure they do" said G

"someone call the waiter, i'm hungry" said J

as L raised his hand and the waiter arrived, he said

"everyone ready to order?"

"order for me the 8 piece salmon sashimi" said JV to G

"i'll have the shrimp tacos" said silicone titted asian A

"i want the grilled octopus" said D

"what about you mam" said the waiter directed to C

"i'll have another moscow mule" said tipsy C

"you should eat something" said silicone titted M

"i'm trying to lose a couple pounds before i get to Big Beach" said C

"the rest of us will have 3 shrimp moquecas, with no dende and bring us another round of drinks" said G

"oh look, i think that's Carlos" said B as he took a better look "it is him, i gonna go talk to him" said B as he got up from the table and went in direction of Carlos' table

"i heard he just finished with his girlfriend, i hope he is going to Big Beach too" said silicone titted M

"he is a good looking dude" said L talking to R

"he is, he is" said R while G shaked his head in agreement

"i'm going to the bathroom, anyone wanna come" said BP

"i do" said R

"any of the girls stupid" she responded

"i'll go with you" said GB

"me too" said J

as soon as they left the table, 3 waiters came with our drinks

"here are your drinks" said the waiter as he placed the drinks on the table

"any other thing we could help" said the waiter

"i think we are good for now" said G

as the waiter left the table, B was coming back from Carlos table

"so, so, is he going to Big Beach?" said silicone titted M

"he is, he just stopped here for lunch" responded B

"i'm gonna hook up with him" said silicone titted M

"no, i will" said silicone titted asian A

"i doubt you girls are gonna say that when you see me sucking his face and grabbing his cock" said JV

"girls, girls, stop with that, he's my friend, i'm the one he will be fucking" said B

"girls, there will be so many good looking guys, i doubt you will even be paying attention to him when you get there" said G

as he said that the girls were getting back from the bathroom

"what did i miss?" said BP

"Carlos is going to Big Beach" said JV

"no way! i'm going to kiss him" said BP

"i'm done with this, anyone wanna go to the beach?" said G

"yeah, let's go" said R

G, R, L, D and MV got up from the table with their drinks and went into the direction of the beach. as they got into the water G said

"this is a nice place, we should come here more often"

"even better with the girls" said D

"those nice toys they brought too are really nice" said R while making tit gestures with his hands

"yeah, like silicone titted asian A's really fitted her, but i think silicone titted M's putted too much" said L

"the thing is she is petite, she didn't need to put 500ml, if she putted silicone titted asian A's size it would be perfect, she would be looking like a princess" said MV

"yeah, she has a nice ass too, i think her silicone was too much" said G "i ain't complaining" said D

"don't get me wrong, it looks nice but i gotta concur with L and MV, she should have putten a smaller size" said R

"i mean, i'm a men and shit and big tits are my thing but it's about fitting the body, if she was taller she would be an absurd with this size, but she is petite" said L

"i would still play with them" said MV

"shut MV, you would play with B's titties" said G

"i saw silicone titted asian A offering her titties for you to play in the car and you denied the lady" continued G

"he did what? let me get a bit further from him before he tries to grab my cock" said D

"the lady wanted him to play with her new toys and MV was just thinking about B at the time, every time we say B he gets a halfy" said R

"that's absurd, you can't be that gay" said L

"i was just trying to not be inelegant, you didn't want me to grab her titties in front of everyone" said MV

"i don't see the problem in that" said G

"me neither" said D

"i'm with G and D, really gay of your part" said R

"you like dick slapping in your face" said L

"my dick to you" said MV

after a while we saw JV coming in direction towards the beach

"the food is here already" she said

"we'll be there in a second" said MV to his sister

while this talk was going on on the beach the girls were having a conversation too. as the guys were walking down the restaurant stairs to the beach BP said

"who would you girls get from the guys?" said BP

without hesitation silicone titted M said

"i would get anyone of them, but D"

then she said

"what about you?"

"oh, L of course, he is such a prince" answered BP

"i would get MV, i think he is so sexy, i even said that he could grab my titties, but he said no, like what the fuck" said silicone titted asian A

"i would get G, i love how he is little and kinda buff" said JV

"what about you GB" said BP

"i wouldn't anyone, i'm dating!" responded GB

"bitch, what about Cristopher" continued BP

"oh, he is different, i heard he had a big dick and i had to try it" said GB

"you slut!" said B

"well i would MV too, i love his broad shoulders, i just imagine myself laying my head on his muscular chest" B continued

"that's true, i would get MV too" said Lipsy C

"what about you M, who would you get?" said C

"well, i think R is really sexy" said M

"and you J?" said BP

"well, i would L too, i love his hair" responded J

"bitch, don't even think about it, he's mine" said BP

"well, if he goes to me, i will get him" said J

as J said that 3 waiters came to the table carrying the food. he placed the shrimp tacos in front of silicone titted asian A, the salmon sashimi in front of JV

"the octopus, where should i put it" said the waiter

"right over there" said silicone titted M

then, as he placed the moqueca down, he said

"be careful with the plate, it is really hot"

"i think i should go call the boys" said JV as she stood up from the table and went in direction of the beach

as she saw the boys on the water she said

"the food is here already"

"we'll be there in a second" responded MV to his sister

as the five of them got to the table and sitted down, BP said

"GB how big was Cristopher really?"

and GB responded

"girl, he was huge, he destroyed my little pussy, it's all fucked up because of him, t he things are out of my pussy, it's all messed up. i'm thinking of doing a pussy recovery surgery, but damn i got all dehydrated because of the water that went out of my pussy"

"you should do the pussy recovery surgery, i heard it makes magic to your pussy" said BP

"yeah, i' think i'm gonna do it, say i'm travelling while i'm doing or something like that" said GB

then she continued

"that's why i came in the first place, i couldn't spend new years with him or he would have seen my pussy all destroyed and know it wasn't him with that small dick, hihihihi"

then BP said

"but tell me about Cristopher, i want to meet him sometime later" "noooo, he's my lover, my big dicked gigolo " responded GB

"you are so possessive" said BP

"you should have seen how dominatrix i was with him, i tied him up and putted a blind fold and then sitted on his dick and went up and down, up and down" said GB

"you are such a crazy slut with that blind fold shit, i like them to look in my eyes while i sit on their cock" said BP

"you don't like that? i mean i don't do it with my boyfriend, but i love doing that to my lover" said GB

"honestly i never tried it" said BP

"it makes me think that i am a queen dominating my servant" said GB

"he is indeed serving you cock" said R

"oh yeah, and what a cock" said GB

as we finished our lunch, Carlos showed up in the table and said

"hey B, hey girls, what's up guys"

"heeeeeeey!!!!" said all the girls at once.

i didn't get the reason why they said hey the way they did, he was good looking and shit but i thought they acted slutty, thought G

bitch one of them got a 500ml silicone tit of course they gonna act slutty, mentally responded r.

"what's up" said the guys

hold on a second, did he just mentally responded him, thought L

it's a metaphor for big dicks, thought D

"we are about to leave to Big Beach, i guess we'll see you girls there" said Carlos.

i should have grabbed silicone titted asian A tits, thought MV

"we will" said silicone titted M

then Carlos left in direction of his boat

"how far from here is Big Beach anyway" said tipsy C

"it's a 2 hour boat ride from here, but i thought we could stop in a private beach on our way and watch the sunset" said G

"you're such a prince G" said silicone titted M

"that's a nice call" said MV

after everyone was done eating the waiter got to our table

"any desserts?" asked the waiter

"i'll have the dulce de leche petit gateau" said silicone titted M

"i don't want anything" said L

"me neither" said R

"i'll have the strawberry cheesecake" said tipsy C

"bitch, weren't you trying to lose pounds?" said BP

"girl, it's just a cheesecake, i sweat this sucking dick" responded tipsy C

"i'll have the brownie with white brigadeiro on top" said silicone titted asian A

"that's a nice dessert" said the waiter

as the waiter left with our order, GB said

"this Carlos is such a dream, if he wasn't friend with my boyfriend i would fuck him too"

"he is, isn't him" said silicone titted M

"he is so handsome, so tall and muscular, i wonder if he got a big dick" said BP

"where is this private beach G" said C

"i don't know man" responded G

then L said

"it probably is somewhere in our way there"

"who ordered the brownie?" said D

"me!" said silicone titted asian A

"can i have a piece?" said D

"why didn't you ordered yours?" said silicone titted asian A "i didn't want a whole one, i just want a piece" said D

"okay" said silicone titted asian A

then B said

"do you think i have a chance with Carlos"

"he is not gay" said BP

"still, like if he is drunk and shit" said B

"straight man don't turn gay, if they are gay they are gay, if they are straight they are straight" said silicone titted M

"he could be bi" said B

"all bi man are gay, they are just more reasonable because they like pussy too" said G

"fuck you" said B

"it's the truth, it hurts to hear" said G

"would you fuck me B?" said BP

"i don't know if my dick would go up, but if you stick a finger up my ass, maybe" said B

"maybe we should try it some time" said BP

"maybe" said B

"have you ever tried pussy B?" said silicone titted M

"i was going to, this one time, but when i placed my face there i didn't like the smell" said B

"i'll put perfume there for you, i'll fuck you straight" said BP

"that's impossible, i like dick too much" said B

"i want to fuck B too" said silicone titted M

"maybe we should all get together and make an orgy with B" said C

"i'm gay too!!!!" said R

"me too" said L

"then kiss guys and we'll have an orgy with you too" said silicone titted M

"no, no, no, no, no" said R and L together

as that happened the waiter got there with the desserts

"the dulce de leche petit gateau for the lady, the strawberry cheesecake for the madam and here is your brownie" said the waiter

as soon as the waiter placed the brownie on the table D got his piece

"ass" said silicone titted asian A

"what happened?" said BP

"he got half of my brownie" said silicone titted asian A

"i didn't know it had brigadeiro on top" said D with a mouthfull

"close your mouth" said silicone titted asian A

so D closed

"thank you" she said

after the girls finished their desserts, the guys payed the check and followed to the boat on the restaurant pier. this time they all went to the upper deck. the boat followed to the private beach where they watched the sunset under the sound of sax house. MV was so animated that he was making sax sounds with his mouths, "piawnnawnawnawpiaww", but beside that they were all quiet just feeling the atmosphere, it was really nice, they went to the lower deck and some of them even got in the water to watch the sunset

. then, as the sun was past gone they followed in the dark toward Big Beach, it didn't have a light to be seen just the stars guiding our way. they sailed and sailed and sailed and then suddenly the boat started to slow down

"i think we are here" said G

then the sailor got to the upper deck and said

"we arrived"

the small boat took us to the shore with our baggages. at the shore there had atvs waiting for us and a pickup truck to take our baggages. we followed the pickup truck to the house by twos. it was a nice house, a contemporary architecture house with 9 rooms in front of the beach, it also had a nice garden with a pool

as the party was a concept house it started early, so we didn't had time to go to the village to have dinner, we only got ourselve s ready to go to the party. the guys got ready first and as they waited for the girls by the pool L said

"i'm gonna get three today" said L

"i was seeing the video of last year, so many hot girls" said G

MV was in that state of kinda of hungover you get when you day drink and stop before start drinking again, so he was quiet. D on the other hand, hadn't come down, he was probably combing his beard, as people with beards probably do

"we should be drinking now, get there sober is bad" continued G.

"yeah, but we didn't had time to buy drinks tomorrow we buy" said R

"it will be a while before this girls are done getting ready, we could go buy and come back and they will still be upstairs" said L "do you wanna go in that mission?" said R

"alone no, but if one of you come with, i'll go. i mean at least some red bull, i need something to get me going" said L

"i think the move is to drink at the party today and tomorrow we buy drinks to drink here" said G

"yeah L, tomorrow we buy" said R

"you two are two lazy fucks" said L

"are you down MV?" he continued

"what? i wasn't paying attention" responded MV

"buy some drinks, get to the party nice instead of getting there sober" said L

"yeah, whatever, let's go" said MV

as they entered the house in direction of the atv, D was coming down the stairs with his beard combed

"who was leaving?" said D

"L and MV, they are going to the village to buy some drinks" said R

"did you tell them to buy water, there isn't water here" said D

"i'll send him a message" said G

"actually, tomorrow we buy there isn't signal" continued G

"i think there's wi-fi here" said R

G stood up from the table and went inside the house

"nice call from L to go buy drinks, the girls won't be down for a long time" said R

then D said

"yeah, but we need water too"

"it would be nice for them to buy some juice too, those pre-made juice cartons" said R as G was coming back

"G tell them to buy some juice" said D

"where will they find juice?" said G

"those pre made juice carton, they probably find them in the drink's place" answered D

"what's the wi-fi" said R

"the name is bbh190 and the password is bbh190123" answered G

as he said that silicone titted M, silicone titted asian A and JV were getting down the stairs

"is there wi-fi here?" said silicone titted M

"the name is bbh190 and the password is bbh 190123" said G

"where is MV?" said JV

"this girl came here asking for him by name and took him to her place" said R

"really?" said JV with a smile

"no, he went to buy drinks with L" responded R

"well we won't wait for them" said silicone titted asian A

"yeah, we want to get there early today" said silicone titted M

"do you even know how to get there?" said G

"no, not really, but maybe you could go with us G" said silicone titted M

"i'll wait for them" said G

"common G, let's go, i'll play with your cock later if you come" said silicone titted M

G looked at R and D for answers and said

"no, no, no, i'll wait for them" said G

"fag, i wouldn't even be able to find your cock without magnifying glass anyway" said silicone titted M as the three girls sitted down

as that happened B, C and M were getting down the stairs talking. as they got outside in the pool front table B said

"is there wi-fi?"

"the name is bbh190 and the password is bbh190123" answered G

"we need drinks!" said C that wasn't tipsy anymore

"L and MV went to the village to buy some" said G

"did you tell them to buy water?" said D

"i texted them" said G

"we can drink at the party, it's open bar, let's go G" said silicone titted M

"we should wait for them, it's a five day party, you will have enough time to chase cock" said G

"her pussy is on fire waiting for some milk to put it out" said B

"and your ass isn't" said silicone titted M sarcastically

"it is, i'm not gonna lie but i can wait 5 minutes for the boys to come back" answered B.

"didn't anyone bring a sound box?" said silicone titted asian A "i brought!" said R as he stood up and went upstairs to get the box

"is it VC today?" questioned C

"no, today is a house concept party" said G

"what does that even mean?" said silicone titted M

"it's a party with a couple djs, but no one is a big name, just really atmospheric" said G as R was coming back the stairs with the sound box. as he got to the table he putted some funk

"sit, sit, sit, sit, sit, sit, sit, sit with your booty in my dick, sit, sit, sit, sit and shake, and shake it, and shake it, shake that booty in my dick, and sit, sit, sit, sit, sit with that booty"

"nooo, put house music" said silicone titted M, so R changed the music "i love this song!" said silicone titted M

"i love cock" said B

after this declaration from B, L and MV was getting back to the house

"we bought gin, vodka and red bull" said MV with a red bull in his hand

"what about the water?" asked D

"no one told me to buy water" said MV

"G texted you" said D

he grabbed his phone and said

"no he didn't"

"you probably didn't have a signal" said G

"so how am i supposed to see the message?" said MV

"that's true, he can't see the message if he doesn't have signal" said silicone titted M

"fuck it, tomorrow we buy" said G

as we poured ourselves drinks and sitted back at the table, it was a nice atmosphere, we could hear the ocean coming and going, coming and going and the sky was bright with so many stars. that's the best part of these places, being able to see the sky you can't see in the city

"would you really play with my cock if i drove you there?" said G

"if i could find that little wormy maybe" said silicone titted M

"it's better this way, you wouldn't be able to walk tomorrow" said G

"i would have a better chance of having an orgasm with the water droplets that falls o n my pussy during my shower" said silicone titted M

"i love when you talk dirty to me, it makes me think of later tonight when you be whipping me with your whip" said G

"ewwwww, that's the porn you gonna watch when you are jerking your dick alone?" said silicone titted M

then R said

"BP, J and GB are still getting ready?"

"that could take a while" said B

"L, MV, how was the village, alot of girls?" asked R

"there had none, po" said L sarcastically

"so many, tomorrow in the beach it will be nice" said MV

"today at the party MV" said G

"true" said MV

"what about guys, did you see any hot ones?" said silicone titted M

"i don't look at guys, but i did see the guy at the store, he seemed like a nice guy, maybe you should go for him!" said L

"ass" she responded

"why you guys gotta be assholes all the time?" said silicone titted asian A

"because if we were nice, you would be with the other assholes" said G

"fair point" said silicone titted M

that made me reflect for a second. because that's a stupid theory, but maybe that is something true. maybe and just maybe, girls like to be slapped in their faces with cock so much that they are sub-consciously attracted to assholes since they know that nice guys respect them too much to slap their faces with cock

as that happened BP, J and GB were coming down the stairs, they looked nice, all the girls looked nice with their outfits

"the girls are ready, can we go now?" said silicone titted M

as we finished our drinks, we got inside the house and went toward the front lawn where the atvs were. we got in the atvs in twos and followed to the party. silicone titted M was on G's back, silicone titted asian A was in MV's back, J on L's, M on R's, B on D's, C on JV's and BP on GB's. as we got near we could hear the loud sound from far

we got to the party, parked outside and waited for everyone to park. when everyone had parked their atv we followed inside. they gave us a silk wristband for the 5 days and then we got inside the party was in this enormous front beach place with lots of palm trees and with sand on the ground and as soon as we got inside we noticed, everyone there was hot, girls and boys

"we are going to go to the bathroom" said silicone titted M

"sounds good, we are going to get some drinks" said G

all the girls went to the bathroom, but B went with the guys to get drinks. we got to the stand and ordered tropical gins, they served us on those huge round gin cups, the guys felt sexy with those cups, it really fitted their outfits

they were wearing havaiana sandals, short beach shorts and black shirts

B and L were wearing a white shirt, but G, R, MV and D opted for black since it makes you look thinner, but white does give a nice look "let's walk around" said MV

so they walked around. the gin bar was on the left from the entrance, from the stage view was on the right, but we weren't on the stage, so it was on the left, there had other bars to the right but it was a beer one, and the guys weren't crazy to be drinking beer or else they were going to be all bloated tomorrow on the beach

but yes, they walked around, saw some girls smiling at them, but it was early so they weren't making moves, but then suddenly they stopped. they took a look why and L was talking to this girl, they were flirting and then they started kissing, tongue on tongue really naughty, then he got her number, gave her a peck on her lips and then they started moving again

but by the time they gave a circle on the party, MV said

"i need to go to the bathroom"

so they went to the bathroom. there they found the girls waiting for someone. MV went in the bathroom with D and L

"where were you guys?" said BP

"we went to get some drinks" said R

"what are you drinking?" said BP

"tropical gin" said R

"can i have a sip?" she said

"yes" said R

so she took a sip

"this is really good" BP said

"where is the bar?" she continued

"right there" R pointed

"we are going to get some drinks, will you guys wait for us?" said BP

"yes" said R

the girls went in direction of the bar, we stayed there waiting for the guys to get out of the bathroom. as the guys got out of the bathroom, L said

"let's go"

"the girls said for us to wait here for them to get drinks" said R

"common man, so many girls here, let's walk around again" said L

"we should wait" said G

so they waited. the girls got back dancing, some where hoping, with their round gin cups spilling all over. C got D hand and started moving it around, D was with a round gin cup too but it didn't fit him right, i think it was the beard. people with beard don't fit with the round gin cups, he should have gotten a beer, it even rhymes, beard and beer

the party was full, but there had still people coming in, hot people after hot people. the group were staying kinda far from the stage, but it was a nice atmosphere there, the sound wasn't too loud

"let's walk around" said L

"let's get a refill first, my cup is about to end" said G

"yeah, let's go" said MV

so they went

"a tropical gin please" said G

so the bartender filled G's cup

"what about you?" said the bartender to MV

"a tropical gin" said MV

after they all gotten tropical gins. they went to the side of the bar. it is a nice place to stay because all the girls go there to fill their cups, so there had a lot of coming and going of hot girls. one of them even smiled at B, she didn't know he liked cock more than her, but how could her?

after she filled her cup, she came talk to B, she was accompanied by 2 other girls. B then suddenly called us, the guys were looking at the stage at that moment

"hey guys, come meet Ana and the girls" said B

the guys turned to the girls and introduced themselves

"hi, nice to meet you, my name is R, this is G, he is MV, he is D and this is L" said R

but R was talking with a sexy voice, it wasn't his normal voice but it sounded good "hey my name is Ana" said Ana smiling

"my name is Laura, and this is Julia" said Laura

"did you girls got here today?" said R

"no, we got here yesterday, we were at the beach all today, look at my tan lines" said Ana as she showed R her tan lines

so G said

"so you girls coming everyday?"

"no, no, no, we are coming today and on new years" said Ana

you poor dirty sluts thought G at that moment

"ohhh, then we gotta enjoy you are here" said R

"yeah, we have too" said Ana smiling

so R and Ana started to kiss

then L pointed to R and Ana kissing and Laura gave a small laugh, so L started to kiss Laura and then G said to Julia

"so are you going to the beach tomorrow?"

"yeah, but we have to think of today"

and then G and Julia started to kiss

when we stopped kissing, we got the girls numbers and G said

"so i guess we see you girls tomorrow in the beach"

then R said

"where is a good place here?"

then Ana said

"today we were at macunacasa, but tomorrow we haven't decided yet"

"tomorrow we text you, so we can do something" said R

"i'll be waiting!" said Ana smiling and then they left to the stage

G then touched MV shoulder and said

"let's walk around"

so MV went on front

we walked pass the stage and gave another circle on the party and then found the girls. silicone titted M was talking about this guy that got her number

"he was so pretty, he looked like a prince!" said silicone titted M

"he really was, his friends were so hot too, are they coming everyday?" said JV "they are! maybe tomorrow we can kiss them, i would have kissed him today, but he was really slow and didn't make a move" said silicone titted M

"i hate when good looking boys are like that, they just don't know what to do" said silicone titted asian A

"that's why i mostly hook up with men, because they know how to do their stuff" silicone titted asian A continued

"yeah that's true, this boys are normally womanish, but they are so pretty!" said silicone titted M

"yeah, maybe tomorrow he text you and we meet them at the beach" said silicone titted asian A

"look the boys are here!" said silicone titted M

"where were you guys?" silicone titted M then continued

"we were at the bar getting drinks" said G

"my cup is almost empty, sometime soon i need to go refill it" said JV

"i'll go with you!" said silicone titted asian A

"you don't have too, either way i still got a bit left in my cup" said JV

JV looked at G and thought, he is looking so pretty today, with his brown hair and compact buff body, this shorts really fits him too. G was wearing a white beach short with flowers on it. so she smiled at him. G noticed she smiled at her and smiled back while he took a sip of his gin through his straw

she blushed and looked away

but then she looked back again

he got near her and said

"this place looks so good" said G

"it does, doesn't it? did you notice the palm trees?" said JV

"i did, and here specially with the stars and the lights from the stage it will be a really nice 5 days" said G

"i also can't wait for the beach tomorrow" said JV

"but we have to enjoy today too" said G

"we do have to" said JV smiling

"yeah, but tomorrow in the beach it will going to be nice. i met this guy in the bar and he was telling me about this place called macunacasa, we should go there" said G

"we could go but tomorrow when we wake up we decide" said JV

"so have you seen anyone you liked so far?" said G

"i did" said JV

"really?" said G kinda bummed out

"yeah, he came with me in the boat" she said smiling

G took a sip of his gin through his straw again, but now he was feeling confident, he didn't know if he should kiss her right there in front of everyone so he said

"i bet he is good looking"

"kinda small, but i kinda like him like that" said JV

now he was sure, but still he didn't know if he should kiss her right there, everyone was watching, so he said

"so why don't you say something to him?"

"i am saying" said JV

so he went to kiss her but she turned her away and whispered in his ears

"not here, everyone is watching" said JV

she smiled and gave him a kiss on his cheek and said

"silicone titted M, silicone titted asian A , i'm going to get some drinks"

"my cup is full but if you want i can go with you" said silicone titted M

"no, i'm going alone" said JV as she looked at G

G waited for a second and when JV was getting to the bar, he went after her. as he got near her he said

"so you are into small dudes?"

JV didn't even say anything, she just kissed him

then she stopped and said

"i am" and then kissed him again

back in the group, B got into R's ears and said

"i want to suck a dick today"

"i hope it isn't mine" said R

MV was vibing in this moment, dancing, just feeling the moment, when he noticed this girl looking at him. she was in a group with some other girls

"D let's go talk to those girls" said MV

"no, i'm good!" said D

"stop being gay, let's go" said MV

"no, maybe later" said D

so MV went to R and said

"R let's go talk to those girls"

"let's go!!!" said R

so MV and R went to talk to the girls

while this was going on, three boys got to the group

"i don't think i've met you yet" said this tall guy, with blonde hair and blue eyes to BP, she smiled and said

"hi, my name is BP"

"hi, BP i'm Lorenzo, but you can call me Enzo"

Enzo was with Henrique and Eduardo

Henrique was talking to C and Eduardo was talking to silicone titted asian A

"did you got here today?" said Enzo

"i did, how about you?" said BP

"yeah, me too. we were in such a hurry to get to the party that we didn't even have time to have dinner, i'm starving here" said Enzo

BP smiled and said

"the same with us, but we were lucky because we stopped in a restaurant in our way here, i wish there had somewhere to eat here"

"there must be a place to get something to eat around here, it is not possible that they only got gin here" said Enzo

"we should go look for food" said BP

"yeah, let's go!" said Enzo

"girls, i'm going with Enzo to get some food" said BP as she left with Enzo to find food

"where you from by the way?" said Enzo

"i'm from here, i mean not here here, but bahia" said BP

"oh, that's nice, it must not even be that much hazzle to get here then" said Enzo

"we just got in a boat. here is 4 hours from salvador. what about you, where are you from?" said BP

"i'm from sao paulo, the other one, the one with brown hair that was with me is from sao paulo too, he is Eduardo, but the mulatto one, Henrique, he is from salvador, well he was born in salvador, but he lives in sao paulo, so we got a plane here and then got into a boat too. by the way, was the restaurant that you stopped in your way here good? it would be nice to have lunch before leaving" said Enzo

"really good! the name is pink oyster. but you are thinking of leaving already and you barely gotten here!" said BP "we are leaving the day after tomorrow, we are spending new years in trancoso with my family, what about you?" said Enzo

"there is a nice place, i was there for new years 2 years ago. i'm gonna be here for new years" said BP

"look, they have tapioca" said Enzo

as they got to the stand, BP ordered a tapioca with cheese and tomatoes, Enzo ordered one with condensed milk

"can i have a bite of your tapioca?" said Enzo

"only if you give me a bite of yours" said BP

"sounds fair" said Enzo

the woman of the stand gave them their tapiocas and they ate their tapiocas. each one got a bite from the other one tapioca "i love tapioca with condensed milk, i would eat it more often if it didn't get me fat " said BP

"you shouldn't worry about that" said Enzo, BP smiled

as they walked back to the group, they found Henrique kissing C and Eduardo kissing silicone titted asian A. at this moment MV and R were coming back too, JV and G where already there, G talking to L and D and JV talking to silicone titted M. as BP and Enzo got there, Henrique said

"did you guys find anything to eat?"

"we found tapiocas" said Enzo

"i'm starving, where did you find them?" said Henrique

"over there by the back" said Enzo

"i think i'm gonna go get one" said Henrique

"i need one too" said Eduardo

"are you coming Enzo?" said Henrique

"i will, just give me a second" said Enzo

then Enzo turned to BP and said

"so i guess we see each other around, what's your number by the way?"

BP gave Enzo her phone and the guys left to get tapiocas

"so???" said silicone titted M

"nothing happened" said BP

"and i'm not gay" said B

"nothing happened, i swear. we just went get tapiocas" said BP "well, as soon as you guys left the girls started kissing the guys, why didn't you kiss him though" said silicone titted M

"he didn't make a move, he did get my number tho. if he texts me, who knows" said BP

"i hate when boys are gay like that" said silicone titted asian A

"girl, you crazy, gay people have attitude" said B

"he wasn't gay, but i would have kissed him, did you see how pretty he was?" said BP

"really pretty!" said B

"he was!" said silicone titted asian A

"so handsome" said silicone titted M

"i need a refill, anyone wanna come?" said G to the guys

"i'll go" said R

as G and R got to the bar they ordered another tropical gin. as the the waiter was finishing to pour them their drinks Ana, Julia and Laura was getting to the bar

"look who's here" said Ana to R

"hey girls!" said R

"where is L?" said Laura

"he's with B and the other guys somewhere, already missing him?" said R

"i am" said Laura

"i'm missing someone's too" said Ana

so R and Ana started to kiss, then Julia said to G

"aren't you going to kiss me?"

so G started kissing Julia too. they kissed and kissed, first a hand one her cheek, the n the hand started to go down and down until it reached her waist and there his hand stayed

when G stopped kissing Julia and opened his eyes, he sees JV. she takes a look at him and Julia, and starts crying

"girls, we'll see you later" said G as he pulled R by the arms

then when G and R were a bit far from the girls G said

"let's grab a beer"

"why did you do that, they are really hot and i don't want to get a beer, tropical gin keeps you thin and it tastes sweeter" said R

"just come" said G

R didn't get a beer, G did though. as R drank his tropical gin in front of the beer bar, R said "so, why were you rude to the girls?"

"so, earlier today, JV was flirting with me and when she went to get a gin, i followed her and we kissed, and now she saw me kissing Julia and started crying" said G

"you know that you can't be doing naughty stuff with girls when you are with girls that are your friend, specially in the first day of a 5 day trip with her" said R

"but Julia was so sexy, plus i didn't think JV would see me kissing with her" said G

"fair point" said R

"anyway, why did you leave the girls, JV was already crying" R continued

"i thought of going talk to her" said G

"so why didn't you go?" said R

"i don't know" said G

then he said

"i probably should talk to her"

"you probably shouldn't, you should let it rest and maybe some other time she forgets this and kiss you again" said R

after he finished his beer he ordered another one and G and R went to the group. JV had stopped crying by then, but she wasn't pleased to see G. G went to talk to JV, but she threw her gin on his face and said

"don't ever talk to me again"

by then, MV was talking to silicone titted asian A

"did you hear about JV and G?" said silicone titted asian A

"what happened?" said MV

"they kissed earlier and then when JV went to get a gin she saw him kissing this other girl" said silicone titted asian A

"he is an idiot and she is stupid" said MV

"why is she stupid?" said silicone titted asian A

"she shouldn't have kissed him, she should have known better" said MV

"how could she know that he would be kissing some slut as soon as she looks the other way?" said silicone titted asian A

"she should have been smarter, look for men that are worthy" said MV

"if he was half as mature as you, she would be fine" said silicone titted asian A

"it's a pitty there are some people that don't think this way" said MV "who would be so stupid?" said silicone titted asian A

"well, i know a japonese that don't think like that" said MV

"i'm korean" said silicone titted asian A while she went to kiss MV

after this, they danced, drank, kissed, but by the time the party was getting to an end they decided to leave. they got to the atvs and went to the house. as soon as they got to the house the girls went upstairs to their rooms. the guys sitted in the table in front of the pool and talked for a second, mostly about how G was stupid, MV didn't say a word

as the hours passed, L went upstairs to his room, then G, then MV. when MV got to his room, he took a shower and brushed his teeth. how could JV be so stupid MV thought. G? he isn't even that good looking, if it was R, i would understand, he thought again. by the time he was done, he turned off the lights, layed on his bed and closed his eyes

he barely opened his eyes with some light that was coming from the door

but then the light was gone

then he felt someone getting in the bed

she layed down and covered herself with the blanket. then she placed her booty close to his dick and started moving and moving her booty. when his dick was hard, he woke up, he saw that she was silicone titted asian A and started to kiss her. he took his shirt off. she took her shirt off. they kissed, then he kissed her neck and started going down until he reached her nipple. he started sucking her tit, and licking her nipple, and after sucking the right tit, he sucked the left, then he started going down, kissing her abs and then he started taking out her short, she raised her booty to help. then he started to suck her pussy, and suck and suck, and then, when she was all wet, he wen t and placed the tip of his cock inside her pussy, then he pulled out, then he putted all in. in and out, in and out, in and out

"ahhhhhhhhhhhhhh" said silicone titted asian A

"hmmm, hmmm, hmmm" said MV

"ahhh ahhhhhhhh" said silicone titted asian A

"hmmmm, hmmmm, hmmm" said MV

"harder, harder" said silicone titted asian A

so he went harder. they fucked, and fucked and then MV cummed in her belly

after that, they both layed down and slept. silicone titted asian A got up in the middle of the night and went downstairs. R and D was still in the table in the front of the pool. she went to the kitchen and opened th e fridge and then she came outside to the pool and said

"isn't there any water here?"

"i told you we needed to buy some water" said D to R

"we need to buy juice too" said R

day 2

MV woke up with the sunlight that was coming through the curtains. he didn't want to wake up, so he turned to the other side, but the room was too bright by then, so he got up. by then he was already alone in the room. he got into the bathroom and brushed his teeth. when he finished he went down to the kitchen and got a cup of water, someone had bought water by then. the guys were in the pool and the girls were no where to be seen. MV went outside to the pool and said

"where is the girls?"

"they went to village to have breakfast" said R as MV sitted by the pool

"i'm starving, have you guys had breakfast already?" said MV

"not yet, we went to the village to buy water and then came back" said R

"we were waiting for you to get up so we could go eat" said G

"i had a huge insomnia last night" said MV

"that's bad, maybe it was the red bull" said R

"ask me who gave me the insomnia" said MV

"hmmmmmmm, niceeeee, who?" said R

"silicone titted asian A, she came by my room last night when i got upstairs and layed next to me" said MV "she was flirting with you since before the boat, of course that was going to happen" said R

"that's true, she even told you to touch her titties" said G

"i came all over her face" said MV

"nice" said G

the sun was hot by then, by the party tonight the guys were all going to be tanned

"i need to get some sun, i want my cheeks red by tonight" said MV

"you can get in the beach, we are starving" said D

i'll go change" said MV

when MV got down from his shower, the guys got out of the pool and got into the atvs to go to the village. when the guys got in the village R said "where are the girls having breakfast?"

"village caffé" said G

so the guys went to village caffé. when we got there the girls were paying their check

"we won't wait for you" said silicone titted M to G

"okay, good morning to you too" said G

"we are going to the beach, when you get there let us know so we can meet" said silicone titted M

"which place are you going?" said G

"i don't know, JV was telling us about macunacasa, we will probably go there" said silicone titted M

after that the girls left to the beach. the guys sitted down on a table and ordered açai bowls and tapiocas. when they were done, they asked the waiter on how to get to macunacasa, the waiter instructed them on the directions and they left to the beach. they got there on the beach club, it was full. there had people on the pool with drinks and music

"should we stay here?" said R

"the girls said that they were going to macunacasa" said G

"i think we should stay here" said L

"stop being assholes, let's go meet the girls" said MV

so we asked the waiter how to get to macunacasa from the beach club. he said to go by the beach and take a right, so the guys did that. we walked and walked and passed by various beachfront restaurant, but we didn't see macunacasa. by the time we reached the last restaurant we saw the name "macunacasa", there had nice house music playing. we didn't see the girls at once so we got insid e and ordered a table. the waiter took us to a private elevated table in front of the bar, as we sitted down the waiter came to us to take our order.

"we'll want the fried calamari, the coconut shrimp, oysters, stuffed mushroom, salmon carpaccio, tuna bites and two rose wines bottle" said G

the waiter left to place the orders and then the guys saw the girls sitted by the sand tanning. L stood up and went tell them that we were there. as L came back, the girls started coming and sitting down

"what did you guys order?" said BP

"some appetizers and rose wine" said R

then G said

"guess who just got here in Big Beach?"

"who?" said L

"Ricardo, he is gonna put his bags in his hotel and is coming to meet us here" said G

"i love Ricardo!" said silicone titted M

then, the waiter got to the table with the two rose wines and poured everyone a cup. by the time he poured everyone a cup the second bottle was about to end

"bring us two more bottles please" said G as he took a sip of his rose wine

"yesterday was nice" said R

"it was" said silicone titted M

"who's playing today?" said silicone titted asian A

"H & JO" said G

"who are they?" said silicone titted M

"they play sertanejo" said D

"i wish it was house again" said silicone titted M

"me too" said silicone titted asian A

"there is going to be djs too, i think" said L

the waiter got to the table with our appetizers, we started eating

"what is this, its delicious" said BP

"tuna bites, let me try one" said G as he got one tuna bite

as we drank and ate, Ricardo was getting to macunacasa with Fat Peter and Ceasar. so Ricardo was this jacked dark chocolate hombre with huge pectoral muscles, broad shoulders and a nice biceps. Fat Peter was also this dark chocolate man, but he was fat. Ceasar was small and thin and didn't look nice but he was Ricardo's friend and Ricardo was the guys friend so the guys didn't say anything

"Riiicardoooooo" said all the girls at once

"ohhhhhhhhh" said G as Ricardo sitted down in the table

"R, do you remember that day in bootsies?" he continued

"how could i forget, hahahahah" said R laughing

"what happened at bootsies?" said BP

"so we get to bootsies right, and we get a table, then i go get some singles on the atm machine and while i'm there this girl asks me if i want a lap dance, so i say yes. so when we are getting back to the table, the girl gets there, sees Ricardo and says 'Riiicardooooo', the guy goes there so much that all the girls know him" said G

"ewwwwww, you guys go to bootsies?" said silicone titted M

"what can i say? it's disneyland for grown ups" said Ricardo

"how can you compare disneyland with bootsies?" said silicone titted M

"have you ever been to bootsies?" said Ricardo

"no" said silicone titted M

"so you don't know what you are talking about, it have ferris wheels, naked girls dancing on poles, i can feel the magic as soon as i get in the door" said Ricardo

"how you doing my dark chocolate bonbon?" said G

"feeling good, just got here, we woke up early so we could get to the beach here today, i should have came yesterday tho" said Ricardo

"how was yesterday at the party" Ricardo continued

"it was good, i got..." G stopped and looked at JV

"it was good" he then said

"nice, i hope today is good too" said Ricardo

"i'm gonna capture Ricardo and put him in my zoo with bubbles" said G

"who is bubbles?" said Ricardo

"my capuchin" said G

"fuck you, you racist" said Ricardo

"i'm not racist my bonbon" said G

"look at what you said" said Ricardo

"i think racism is stupid, how can someone judge someone by their skin color and not based on what is in their mind" said G "you still can't say you are going to put me in a zoo with a capuchin, is basically calling me a nigga" said Ricardo

"i don't know what's up with that either, why don't black people just call white people snowflakes or baby powder when that happens" said G

"it's not the same" said Ricardo

"doesn't being offended by someone calling you nigga imply that this person think that the word nigga carries a bad connotation, why isn't nigga something good, like you are my nigga man mean like you are this superguy instead of something bad" said D

"only black people can say nigga" said Ricardo

"isn't that confusing? like the same word meaning good when it comes from one group and bad when it comes from another group of people. like imagine good meaning good when someone says good and bad when someone else says it" said R

"isn't that racism?" said G

"in this table the only people that can say nigga is me and Fat Peter" said Ricardo

"can i call you my nigga?" said silicone titted asian A

"you can, but it's because you're sexy" said Ricardo

"i'll call you my dark chocolate bonbon" said G

"that's calling me a gay nigga" said Ricardo

then silicone titted M said outloud

"do you wanna get married?"

"i mean married married no, but like living together and have kids yeah, marriage is a scam where you sign a piece of paper and a girl takes half of what you own" said R

"i wanna get married, live together and have lots of kids" said silicone titted M

"i think living together is weird, like two people living together in the same home, like what the fuck, imagine having half a bed every day and not even fucking most of the time" said D

"you don't fuck because you don't want too" said silicone titted M

"i'm not going to rape my wife" said D

"yeah, but if she doesn't want to fuck you is because you are doing something that is not making her happy, you gotta buy her diamonds, like a lot of diamonds" said silicone titted M

"i want to get married and live together, me and Roberto are going to live together and adopts 3 children, 2 of them are going to be blacker than Ricardo and one is going to be vietnamese" said B

"i want a girl that is a roommate that can't pay her rent, so i pay for her and then she owes me but she can't pay me with money so she pays me with her pussy" said MV

"so you want a sex puppet?" said G

"when you put like that its kinda mean, i rather put it like a roommate that can't pay her rent" said MV

as that was going on, the rose wine was about to end, so G called the waiter and said

"two more rose wine bottles per favore"

as the waiter brought the two bottles and poured down the wine cups BP said

"guess who just texted me"

"who?' said silicone titted asian A

"Enzo, he told me to go to his place and bring you and C" said BP

silicone titted asian A looked at MV and said

"i'll go"

"me too" said C as they stood up

the girls went through the restaurant door were they parked their atv. the three of them got in the same atv and went to Enzo's house. they didn't know exactly where it was but they eventually found it. it was a beach front house, huge and the 3 boys were the only ones staying there. they got in by the garden. Enzo was on the couch with his phone and Eduardo and Henrique on the pool. Enzo got up from the couch and said

"hey BP!"

"hi!" said BP

"you must be silicone titted asian A" Enzo said while giving a kiss on her cheek

"hi!" said silicone titted asian A

"and you C" said Enzo while giving her a kiss on the cheek

"hi!" said C as the other guys got up from the pool

"you girls want to drink something?" said Eduardo

"i'll have a gin and tonic" said silicone titted asian A

"me too!" said BP

"the same!" said C

Eduardo went inside and got some cups while Henrique opened the fridge outside the house and took the gin and tonic. as Eduardo got back with the cups, Enzo said "was the beach nice?"

"it was full of people, really beautiful the beach here" said BP

"you girls must come here alot, so close to home" said Enzo

"we actually live in miami, but we come here now and then, what about you guys, first time here?" said BP as they sitted down on the couch

"mine yes!" said Enzo

"actually, i've come here when i was a kid but i was too young and it doesn't count" he continued

"it's my first time too" said Eduardo

"i come here every year with some friends and now i'm bringing this two" said Henrique

"so is this house yours?" said C

dont poke the condom whore, thought Henrique

"it is, me and my family spend new years here every year but this year we are going to trancoso" said Henrique

"i love trancoso, we went to new years there 2 years ago" said C

"yeah BP told me. me and Eduardo go to new year there every year, funny how we never met" said Enzo

"sometimes the universe is waiting for the right place for some people to meet" said C

"trancoso is beautiful too, but i think the girls here are more beautiful" said Enzo

"hey silicone titted asian A, do you want to go to the pool?" said Eduardo

"yeah, let's go" said silicone titted asian A as she stood up with her drink and went in the direction of the pool "i think i'm gonna go to the pool too, are you coming Enzo?" said Henrique

"i think i'm gonna stay here" said Enzo as Henrique and C got up and followed Eduardo

"so, trancoso" said BP

"when are you going?" BP continued

"tomorrow" said Enzo

"plane or helicopter?" said BP

"helicopter, we taking a boat to salvador and meeting my family there and then we get the helicopter and go" said Enzo

"why don't they get you here" said BP

"my parents are coming from sao paulo by plane, we are going to meet them at the airport and heading there" said Enzo

"i'm scared of helicopters" said BP

"why? they take you where you wanna go really fast" said Enzo

"that's true, but i prefer planes, like if a plane falls the pilot can ajust something and you have a better chance of surviving but if the helicopter have a problem it just falls and you die" said BP

"you know i'm getting in a helicopter tomorrow right?" said Enzo

"i'm just trying to make you stay" said BP

"you say that but you haven't even kissed me yet" said Enzo

BP turned to Enzo and kissed him sideways, then he placed his hands went on her thighs and she climbed on top of his lap. as this happened, in the pool henrique said

"see that his not gay"

"still, he could be bi" said C

"he just don't kiss girls on party" said Henrique

"which means his more gay than straight" said C

"maybe he has a girlfriend" said silicone titted asian A

Henrique looked at Eduardo at this time and said

"he doesn't"

"then what's the problem of kissing someone in the party" said silicone titted asian A

"you just don't kiss someone in front of other people if you are hiding something" said C

"i don't know what to say, but he doesn't have a girlfriend" said Henrique "we will pretend that we believe that" said C

"who dates nowdays anyway?" said silicone titted asian A

"if you find someone special wouldn't you girls date?" said Eduardo

"like exclusively? no, at least not now" said silicone titted asian A

"i have to come more often to bahia" said Eduardo

"you guys in sao paulo dates alot?" said C

"depend of the person" said Henrique

"i think we have to enjoy our youth, soon we will be old and then what, you wasted a long time dating someone that is not even in your life anymore" said silicone titted asian A "but what if that is the person you spend your life with" said Eduardo

"yeah, so you spend a long time with them until they realize how sexy his secretary is and decide to fuck her" said silicone titted asian A

"who broke you girls?" said Eduardo

"we just know how it is, sooner or later our body won't be tight anymore" said C

"plus, exclusivity is boring" said silicone titted asian A

while this was going on, Enzo turned to BP in the couch and said

"wanna go upstairs?"

"let's go" said BP

as Enzo went upstairs with BP, they got in the first room on the right. it was a large room made up with wood. they started kissin g again, Enzo took his shirt off while still standing. BP were wearing a long beach skirt and a bikini top, so Enzo started kissing her neck and going down. when he reached her breast, he pulled her bikini top down and started kissing her breasts. she stopped for a second and took her skirt off and then took her bikini top off. Enzo took her to the bed and continued kissing her. he continued going down her abs and down and down until he reached her pussy. he sucked her pussy, then he stopped for a second and pulled his shorts and underwear off. he then pushed her bikini bottom to the side and put his dick inside. in and out, then he went harder and harder. then BP pulled him to a stop, took her bikini bottom out and said

"now it's my turn"

Enzo layed on his back and BP got on top of him and started moving and moving on top of Enzo. she then squatted on top of him with her hands of his pectoral muscles and started moving and moving. Enzo then said "i'm gonna cum"

"i want you to cum on my face" said BP

they stood up BP got on her knees and started to suck Enzo's dick, then he cummed in her face. her face was all white by then. then she licked some of the cum that was on her face and went into the bathroom to wash the rest. when she was done cleaning herself, Enzo was dressed on his shorts but shirtless. he put his shirt on and they went downstairs. the girls weren't at the pool anymore, neither the boys. BP and Enzo got into the pool and stayed there. by then the sun was setting and the sky was orange and purple

while this was going on, everyone was still back in the beach in macunacasa

"if your wife had cancer would you still fuck her?" said silicone titted M

"would she be bold?" said R

"yes" said silicone titted M

"then no, i would get a mistress!" said R

"but what if the doctor says that fucking her helps cure her" said silicone titted M

"then i would hire a gigolo, hey GB what's Cristopher's number again?" said R

"do you remember that day at ocean pepper?" said G

"it was a nice day" said R

"what's the name of that rio girl you was with?" said G

"Sarah, she is such a babe" said R

"didn't you go home with her?" said G

"i did, but we just slept together, we didn't fuck" said R

"i hope the dolphins wins this year" said L

"i'm putting some money on them, the team is good this year" said D

"imagine that, the city will be nuts" said G

"i don't know why you guys like american football so much, the best games end with a guy kicking a ball, why don't just watch soccer" said Ricardo

"i don't care about how the game is gonna be, i care about how crazy the city is gonna be" said G

"you guys didn't say if you guys liked my nose job" said GB

"it looks nice" said MV

"if i was a girl i would do a nose job too, have my nose looking all small and up high" said L

"didn't you do a nose job MV?" said G

"he did" said JV

"hey guys, i think i'm gonna go home to take a nap before the party, let's pay the check for what we got until now, then you guys can continue here" said L

"comon man, you have a nice nose" said R

"is not that, not that, i'm tired" said L

R raised his hand and called the waiter making the check signal, when the waiter got there R said

"he is going to leave now, but we are going to stay here a bit longer but we are going to pay the check and whatever we get from now on you put on a separate tab"

"sounds good" said the waiter as he handed the check to R

R gave a look and passed around as he grabbed his wallet

"should we split it?" said Ricardo

"yeah let's do it" said G

then the tab got to Ceasar and he said

"hey guys, i just had a water, i don't think it's fair for me to split it" said Ceasar

everybody looked at each other and G said

"fine"

we payed the check, Ceasar payed for a water and then L stood up and left in direction of the atv through the beach. Ricardo stood up too and said

"we about to leave too, gonna rest for a second before the party" so Fat Peter and Ceasar also stood up and went to the restaurant door. as they left the restaurant G said

"did Ceasar really just pay for a water?"

"he did, we should tell Ricardo to not bring him next time" said D

as this was going on, the guys and the girls stayed in the restaurant

"two more bottles please" said G

L went walking through the beach to get to his atv. he walked and walked and saw girls tanning and guys playing soccer. the sky was orange and purple, the ocean of blue and reflecting the sky colors. the sun was setting, but the night was still young. when he got to the beach club, in front there had people paying volei with their feet. he got in and a party was going on. he passed by the party and went to the entrance of the beach club where the atv was parked. we should have stayed in the beach club, he thought when he got to the atv, he turned it on and went in the direction of the house. when he got to the house, he parked the atv in the lawn and went inside. he thought he was alone but when he got inside J was in the couch on her phone

"didn't you go to the beach?" said L

"i stayed here in the pool with M" said J

"where is she?" said L

"she went to the village to get a açai bowl with the girls" said J

"which girls?" said L

"little S and some other girls" said J

"where any of them hot?" said L

"not hotter than me" said J

"that is something that is hard" said L

"you just say that because you want to fuck me" said J

"who isn't?" said L

"B" said J

"with that ass, even he would fuck you" said L as he sitted on the couch

"so how was the beach?" said J

"it was nice, the place we went was really good but we should have went to the beach club, it was like really full" said L

"was there having a party there?" said J

"it was" said L

"the girls where there earlier" said J

"we should have went there" said L

"why didn't you go to the beach?" said L

"i don't know, i wanted to relax a bit before tonight" said J

"where are the guys?" said J

"they stayed at the beach, i wanted to take a nap before the party" said L

"so they are not going to come for now?" said J

"not right now" said L

as he said that she got closer to him and placed her hand on his lap

"and i'm the one that want to fuck you" said L

"i didn't say i didn't want to fuck you" said J

as she said that they started to kiss. they kissed for a while then L stood up holding her hand and went upstair to his room when they got there he took his shirt off and started kissing her. she was wearing a bikini. she started to go down on him and pulled his short down. as she did this she started sucking his dick. she spitted on his dick and continued. then he pulled his dick off her mouth, held her head with both hands and started to mouth fuck her really hard

she was gagging

"aghhhhhhhaghhhhhhaghhhhhhh" said J

then he stopped, pulled his dick out and slapped his hard cock on her cheek. right cheek, then left cheek, then right cheek, then left cheek, then left cheek, then right cheek. he was giving her a cock spanking. then he stopped, and slapped his cock on her nose. then he slapped his cock on her right cheek again, then on her forehead, then on her forehead again

then he putted his dick on her mouth again and mouth fucked her once more "do you like it, do you like it my little whore" said L

"aghhhhhhhaghhhhhhaghhhhh" said J gagging

then when he stopped, she got up and took her bikini top out, then her bikini bottom. they went to the bed and L adjusted her on doggy position and started to fuck her. he was pulling her hair backward while he fucked her

"ahhhhhh ahhhh ahhhhhh" said J

"harder harder" said J

L pulled out and went to put it on her ass

"not there, there hurts" said J

so L putted on her pussy once more and started fucking her again. then he pulled out and layed on the bed once more

"suck my dick" said L

so J went and started sucking his dick once more. then she spitted on his dick again and jerked it a bit more so the spit would be all over his dick. then she got in reverse cowgirl position and started sitting on his cock. L then said

"wait a second"

L went inside his bathroom and came back with an argan oil bottle. he layed down on the bed and put a bit of argan oil on his dick and jerked a bit for it to get all over his dick. then J got on top of him but now looked on his eyes as she sitted. she sitted and started moving around

"wowww, this is so good" said J

she sitted and moved, then L put her on doggy position again, put some more argan oil on his cock and fucked her once more like that, then he pulled out and cummed on her back as this happened they heard some music coming from downstairs

"the guys are here" said J

"i guess they are" said L

"just don't tell no one" said J

"i won't" said L as J put her bikini on and left L's room for her room

as J got to her room, G, R, D and MV got in the pool with some drinks. BP, silicone titted asian A and C were already back from Enzo's. silicone titted M and JV sitted in the pool front table with the sound box and after a moment the other girls joined them

"so you are telling me that you only eat protein?" said MV

"not protein, just red meat, that's why the name is the carnivore diet" said C "yesterday you ate rice with the moqueca" said D

"yeah, but it's new year, but all year around you just eat red meat" said G

"what about eggs, eggs are protein" said R

"you can eat eggs, but it's better if you eat only red meat" said G

"so all year around you don't eat one risotto?" said R

"no" said G

"that's insane, don't you miss carbs?" said R

"not a bit, since i started doing this my mood is better, my energy is better, i can carry more weight in the gym and my body looks way better" said G

"what about pizza?" said D

"pizza is not protein" said G

"it got cheese, cheese is protein" said D

"yeah, but it got carbs, you can only eat protein" said G

"hold on a second, you are telling me that you wake up and cook a steak" said MV

"i do" said G

"why don't you eat eggs and bacon like normal people" said MV

"because it have to be red meat, just think of lions, they are the king of the jungle and what do they eat? red meat. they don't eat carbs, they don't eat vegetables, they don't eat eggs, they don't eat chicken, only red meat" said G

"i'm pretty sure lions eat chicken" said R

"they could, but they don't like it" said G

"how do you know what a lion like or doesn't like?" said R

"you eat like them, you start to think like them" said G

"wait, no vegetables too?" said MV

"no, just red meat, i mean i eat fruits too but it's because they taste good" said G

"when i go back to miami i'm gonna give it a try" said MV

"do try it, your body is gonna get insane, trust me" said G

"we should do a barbeque" said D

"who should we call?" said R

"i don't know" said D

"it could be us, these girls, the girls from the party yesterday, little S is here too

, so her with her friends and Ricardo and the guys" said G

"do we need to invite Ceasar?" said D

"he came with Ricardo, so i'm afraid so" said G

"i like that, i haven't seen little S yet, but we should do something about Ceasar" said MV

"like what?" said R

"i don't know, we could hire a prostitute to fuck him while he have the barbeque" said MV

"do you know any prostitutes that are here" said R

"no" said MV

"fuck, if we send the boat to the city tonight i could get one here by later today so she can do that" said D "where would she stay?" said G

"we could get her an hotel here" said MV

"i don't know if we would be able to find one, it's new year, everything is full" said R

"we could try" said D

"let's call and if we find one we do that" said G

"text the girl tho and make sure she is ready to go later today" said R

"hey girls, what do you think of doing a barbeque here during the day tomorrow" said G

"it could be fun" said silicone titted asian A

"can we call Henrique and his friends?" said C

"who's Henrique?" said G

"a friends of ours" said C

"sure" said G

BP turned to C and said

"i think they leave tomorrow morning"

"actually, nevermind. they leave tomorrow morning" said C

"who would come?" said silicone titted M

"us, you girls, Ricardo and little S and her friends" said G

"we need more guys" said silicone titted M

"i don't know any more guys here" said G

"why don't we go to the beach club, they have parties there every day" said BP "we kinda wanted to do a barbeque, but if you girls don't want to we can go to the beach club" said G

"no it's fine, we can do a barbeque tomorrow, but we should go someday to the beach club" said BP

"we'll go someday, can you get our phones" said G

"yes, sure, just yours?" said BP

"no, grab all of them" said G

she got up and brought us our phones. then we searched for hotel numbers and started to call

"i'll call this one, the seahorse hotel" said R

"i'm calling the big beach hotel" said MV

"all sold out" said R

"same here" said MV

we called and called. until D looked at us with a smile and said

"oh, you guys do have a room... ... uhumm... can you guys make a reservation for me?... i'll pass by there now and pay for the room, thank you very much, i'll see you in a bit" said D

D then turned to the guys and said with a big smile

"i'm gonna go there pay for the room, i'll be back in a bit", then he left in direction of the front lawn where the atvs were parked

"i was thinking here and how are we going to make him fuck the prostitute?" said R

"maybe she could grab his cock on breakfast " said G

"we gotta tell Ricardo to not tell him about the barbeque though" said MV

"i don't think grabbing his cock is the right move" said R

"so what do you suggest?" said G

"i was thinking about a love story, something romantic" said R

"oh, hold on a second, i think i have the answer. we ask Ricardo where they are going to have breakfast and then we tell her to go there and spill juice on him. then she says 'oh, i'm so sorry, the least i can do is help you clean your shirt, where is your room' then when they leave we tell Ricardo to come" said R

"it could work" said G

"i like that" said MV

as that was going on, the girls started going upstairs to get ready for the party. so G said

"we should go get ready too"

"i'm gonna finish this drink and go" said R

after they finished their drinks they got out of the pool and went upstairs to get ready. first L got down the stairs, then R, then G, then MV and just then D. the girls were still getting ready

"how do you take so long D, you don't even have hair to put shampoo on" said MV

"i was combing my beard" said D

"how does these girl take so long, they got upstairs first than we did" said G

"i don't know, they don't have a beard to comb" said D

then B got down on his beach shorts and white shirt. L was using the same outfit too. the other guys were using beach shorts and black shirts. music was playing and the guys were having a drink

Ricardo then got to the house with Fat Peter and Ceasar. he doesn't even know the present we got for him, thought MV

"by the way, Ricardo is coming with us today" said G as Ricardo and the other guys took a sit

"where can we get cups" said Ricardo

"inside by the kitchen" said G

Ricardo and the other guys got up and headed to the kitchen where they got cups. they poured themselves drinks and then they took a sit

"who is playing today?" said Ricardo

"H & JO" said L

"the best day" said G

"tomorrow is the best day" said L

"who is tomorrow?" said D

"little T" said G

"tomorrow is the best day" said D

"VC is the best day" said R

"you look like the girls with that house music" said D

"you that look like a construction worker not liking house music" said MV

"i like when people sing, there's emotion, feels human not like a robot" said D

"there are vocals on house music too" said MV

"samba is the best though" said L

"to get girls yes, but to vibe, house music is better" said R

"you crazy, sertanejo is the best to get girls" said G

"both of them are good to get girls" said L

"funk is good to get girls too" said D

"no it isn't, funk is to dance like a petite black girl, those with ripped abs" said Ricardo

"fair point" said D

"by the way, do you remember chick chick on amargosa?" said MV

"those parties in the country are nice" said D

"they are, but, we've outgrown them, now our parties are by the beach" said R as R said that the girls started to come down the stairs in small groups. they poured themselves drinks and sitted down. when everyone got downstairs, we finished our drinks and went toward the front lawn where the atvs where

today, there had more people so some people went on threes. we parked our atvs outside the party and went in, the silk wristband they gave us on the first day served for the 5 days so we just showed them and got in

when we got in silicone titted M said

"we are going to the bathroom"

we went get drinks, we then returned to the front of the bathroom to wait for them. they got out of the bathroom a few at a time and went get drinks. a dj was playing, H & JO was later. when they got back with their tropical gins, C said

"hey B, is Carlos coming today?"

"he probably is" said B

L then turned to G and said

"let's walk around"

"lets" said G

so we went to give a walk around. we passed by the gin bar then went to the front of the stage. when we got to the front of the stage, this girls looked at MV, so we stopped. we went to talk to them

"hi" said MV

"hi" said the girl

"what's your name" said MV

"Maria" said Maria

"what's your name" said L to the other girl

"i'm Bia" said Bia

R was talking to this other girl named Livia and D was talking to Mariana. there had only four girls so G stayed there by the side sipping his tropical gin by the straw. sometimes he looked at the guys talking, sometimes he looked at the stage

"are you girls doing anything tomorrow?" said R

"we are going to the beach, you guys doing something special" said Maria

"we having a barbeque, you girls should go" said L

"maybe we'll go, if we don't find no one better looking" said Maria

"that is going to be something hard to do" said MV

"cocky" said Maria

"am i lying?" said MV

"no, i like it that way anyway" said Maria

"get our numbers then and text the time and place, maybe we show up" said Bia

MV got Maria's phone and said

"were you girls here yesterday?" said MV

"we were, shame that we didn't meet you guys" said Maria

"how do you know we were here yesterday?" said MV

"you guys are suspicious" said Maria

"do you like H & JO?" said MV

"i do, do you know when they start?" said Maria

so i tried to translate this to english but it kinda of doesn't have an accurate translation to how absurd this sounds when saying this to someone you are trying to get but i t kinda means like really sarcastically saying, probably later

"provavelmente mais tarde né porra" said MV kinda of laughing with his hands open like Mbappe celebration where he opens his arms before crossing his arms

"you're mean" said Maria laughing

"that was stupid anyway" she said

he then realized how absurd that sounded so he said

"no, no, no, like they could have cancelled " said MV

"that's even worst" said Maria

"i'm sorry, i just wanted to say that i wanted to be with you in the time that they sing 'i came to end your party life'" he said in the music rhythm i know what it seems, that he is about to murder her, but in portuguese sounds better

"you are unbelievable" she said with a smile, so MV kissed her. L kissed Bia too, R kissed Livia too and D kissed Mariana too

they then continued walking around. when they gave a circle around the party they returned to the front of the bathroom where the girls were. Enzo was there with his friends talking to the girls and Carlos was there too with his friends talking to B and some other girls. when the guys got there this girl touched R's back and said

"my friend thinks you are cute"

"why don't she come tell me that?" said R

"she is shy" said the girl, so R went talk to the girl's friend

after a while H & JO started playing. MV did find the girl when H & JO were ending their show "i didn't see you when they played party life" said MV

"they are playing now" said Maria

"no they aren't, ohhhh" said MV

"just kiss me" said Maria, so MV kissed her

after H & JO finished playing, a house dj got in stage and played for a bit. when the sun was rising, a funk dj got in the stage and played funk. the atmosphere was insane, the sun hitting people's head, with the blue sky on top and the palm trees details. then the music stopped and everyone started to leave. when they got to the atvs, MV said

"i think we should go to the village to eat something"

"let's go" said D

so they went to village caffé and had açai bowls, tapiocas and sandwiches, the girls where there with Enzo too

"what time are you leaving" said BP

"the boat gets here at noon" said Enzo

"we gotta do something before you guys leave" said BP

"you girls want to go to the beach?" said Enzo

"i'll go" said BP

"me too" said silicone titted asian A

"the same" said C

so they got up and went to the beach, while the rest of the group stayed to finish breakfast. after they finished having breakfast, they got up and left to their house

day 3

R was the last to wake up. when he got up from bed he went to the window and opened the curtains so the whole room was bright. he then showered and brushed his teeth. then, he went downstairs. when he got downstairs the girls where in the couch talking, the guys were in the pool

"finally" said G

"we were waiting for you to wake up so we can go to the village buy the things for the barbeque" said MV

"let's go then, let me just drink a cup of water" said R

R went to kitchen and drank a cup of water, then the 5 of them headed to the front lawn to get the atvs. when they got to the village MV said "we'll go buy the drinks and you guys go buy the meat"

so R, D and L went buy the meat. when they got to the place that sells meat R said

"what should we buy?"

"sirloin, ribeye and hump steak" said D

"but hump steak is hard to cook" said R

"then don't buy hump steak" said D

"it's hard to make it like they do it on the brazilian steakhouses" said R

"don't buy it then" said D

"we should buy lamb" said L

"lamb is good" said R

"so buy lamb" said D

"should we buy ribs?" said L

"cooking ribs is hard" said R

"then let's not buy ribs, do you guys like chicken wings?" said D

"i do like it, but i'm not in the mood for chicken wings" said R

"we need sausages" said L

"we should get some vegetables in case some one is vegetarian" said D

"i ate this crocodile this one time, it tasted like fish" said R

"are you kidding me, you wanna have a crocodile barbeque?" said D

"no, i just said that i ate a crocodile this one time, you know what i want?" said R

"what" said D

"i want to have a crocodile belt and three wifes" said R

then L said

"we should get salmon too"

"shrimp maybe" said R

"maybe, do you think we can find octopus?" said D

"maybe, but not here" said R

"we should buy bread, garlic and mayonaise for the garlic bread" R then said

"they don't sell this here, we have to go to the other store" said L

"let's get the meat and then we go buy the garlic bread ingredients" said R

"let's go look for the octopus too" said D

they payed for the meat, then they went to the other store and bought the garlic bread ingredients. the store that sold octopus and salmon was far away so the three didn't go buy them. they also bought apples and carrots in case anyone was vegetarian. when they left the store, the guys couldn't find MV and G on the village so they went to the house. midway there they remembered to buy charcoal, so they went back to the village and bought charcoal. when they got to the house G and MV were in the pool front table having a drink, D joined them. R got the garlic bread ingredients and started preparing them, while L started the grill. when the garlic bread was ready R took them to L but the fire was not good yet so L decided to not put them on the grill just yet. then, Ricardo got to the house with Fat Peter and Ceasar, the plan hadn't worked

"it didn't work" said G

"i know, but don't be unpolite" said MV

"i'm not an animal" said G

"did you hired a toothless whore?" said MV

"no, she is good looking, look at the pictures" said D showing MV the pictures

"still, you could have done better" said MV

"next time, i'll let you hire the prostitute" said D

"i'm just saying, you could have done better" said MV

"do you know how hard it is to find a prostitute in one day on new years" said D

"no, not really" said MV

"then don't say that i could have done better" said D

"i'm just saying" said MV

"i bet he gets the sirloin and runs" said G

"really high probabilities on that" said MV

"now shhhh, he is coming" said G

as Ricardo, Fat Peter and Ceasar got to the table G said

"hey what's up Ricardo"

"what's up" said Ricardo

"what's up guys" said Ceasar

"what's up" said the guys

"is it going to be just us?" said Fat Peter

happy to see that there is going to have a lot of meat for you fatty, thought MV but he said

"little S is coming too"

"i forgot she was here with the girls" said Fat Peter

you only don't forget to eat free willy, thought G but then he said

"Julia is coming with the girls too"

"who is Julia?" said MV

"a girl from the house concept party" said G

"ohhhh, i should call Maria" said MV

"you should talk to R and L first, they got Julia's friends" said G

"and what does that have to do with me" said MV

"i'm just saying they got them and Maria's friend, don't you think its going to be weird that these two groups be here together" said G

"do you hear yourself? you are saying that you can call your girl but i can't call mine" said MV "i'm just saying that you should tell R and L" said G

"that's stupid, they won't even notice that, it's not like the girls will be grabbing their dick in front of everyone" said MV

"just ask them" said G

"i won't ask them" said MV

as he said that L came to the table with the garlic bread, layed it down in the table, got one garlic bread and returned to the grill where R was

"are any of you a vegetarian?" said D

"i'm strictly on a pussy diet" said Ricardo

"someone should go ask the girls, i asked them so its somebody else turn" said D

"we have apple and carrots though" said MV

"we still need to ask them, because if no one is, then we don't need to occupy grill space with the apples" said D

"i don't think we grill apples" said G

"carrots then, all the same thing" said D

"i'll text them" said G as he grabbed his phone

"they said they want fish" said G

"well, we don't have fish" said D

"should we go buy some?" said MV

"the fish store is far away, i wanted some octopus too, but it was too far" said D

"well, give them apple and carrots" said MV

"what if they don't want apple and carrots?" said G

"wait a second, i'm gonna ask if they want apple and carrots" G then continued

"they told me to go fuck myself, that they aren't horses" said G

"someone need to go buy fish then" said MV

"Ceasar you should go with G" said D

"why do i have to go?" said G

"i bought the meat, it's only fair that you buy the fish" said D

"i'll go but you guys need to chip in" said Ceasar

"are you deaf, we bought the meat, what did you bring beside your ugly face" said D

"that's true" said Ceasar

"why do i have to go, why don't MV go" said G

"i ain't your dad, you guys decide" said D

"you cheated on my sister" said MV

"we weren't dating, beside that was like two days ago" said G

"still, i didn't cheat on yours" said MV

"she is 6 for god sake" said G

"well, my sister is 2 for kissing a dwarf, by the way that's true you are a dwarf, dwarfs like buying fish, i'm just respecting your culture" said MV

"guys, you don't want to let Ceasar wait, who got more girls yesterday?" said D

"i got 2" said G

"i got 3" said MV

"you are a dwarf, you cheated on my sister and you got less girls yesterday, sounds like fish buyer to me" said MV "i'm disgusted by fish" said G

"so don't stick it up your ass" said MV

"fine, i'll go" said G

G and Ceasar got up and headed to the front lawn where they would get the atv and go. a bit after L went to the table with a plate of meat

"sirloin" said L and the guys got a piece of the meat

then he went to the couch where the girls were staying and offered them the sirloin, some of them got a piece but some didn't. when he left that area silicone titted M got up from the couch she was sitting and went to the table where the guys were

"isn't no one going to get us some fish"

"G went to buy some fish, didn't you see them leaving?" said Ricardo "he didn't asked us what kind of fish we wanted" said silicone titted M

"he will probably get some salmon" said Ricardo

"maybe some octopus too" said D

"do you think there's signal? we want some shrimp too" said silicone titted M

"probably not, but maybe he buys" said D

"do send him a message though, maybe it gets through" said Ricardo

she texted him while she stood up in front of the table. then went back inside to where the girls were. a while later Ana, Julia and Laura got to the house. they went inside and talked to R and L in the side of the grill

"hey" said Ana

"hi" said R

"so is chef models a thing now" said Ana

"that's all on L, i did made a garlic bread but i'm afraid that it is all done" said R

"some other time you make for me" said Ana

"some other time" said R

"do you girls want some meat, there is a ri beye coming out now" said L

"i'll have a piece, but i like it not too r aw and not too grilled" said Laura

"you'll have to wait a bit then, its raw ri ght now, but afterward i'll grill it a bit more for you" said L

"where is G?" said Julia

"he went to buy fish, some of the girls are vegetarian" said L the girls got a drink and stayed by the side of the grill talking to R and L. a moment later Maria, Bia, Livia and Mariana got to the house. they passed by the table where the guys where staying and they talked to the guys, then Maria and Mariana got a drink and sitted down, while Bia and Livia went to talk to R and L

they talked to them and then got a drink and sitted down on the table where Maria and Mariana were

G then came back with Ceasar, with salmon, tilapia, octopus and shrimp and gave them to L to cook and G stayed by the side of the grill talking to Julia while Ceasar took a sit on the table

a moment later little S got there with her friends, Leticia, Gabriela and Ana Beatriz. they talked to everyone, got a drink and sitted down on the table. a moment later the girls that were staying at the house stood up from the couch inside and went outside inside the pool. the guys too, little S and her friends too and Maria and her friends too, the only people that wasn't on the pool was R, L, G, Ana, Julia and Laura that were in the grill talking while L grilled the fish and the meat

sometimes L, sometimes R, sometimes G would go and serve the people in the pool the fish and meat and sometimes the people on the pool would get out to get another drink and pass by the grill and get a piece of meat. after everyone was done eating, L, R, G and the girls joined the rest of them on the pool. they stayed there the whole afternoon drinking and talking. people then started to leave in groups. first was little S and her friends. then BP, GB and J went upstairs to rest for the party later, then Maria and her friends, then B and the girls also went upstairs. then, Ana and her friends left. then Ceasar and Fat Peter left to go to their hotel, but Ricardo stayed

so in the pool was R, G, MV, D, L and Ricardo. they stayed there talking and drinking and then Ricardo said "i'm going to go to the hotel, see you guys at the party" while he got out from the pool

"can you go upstairs and get the sound box charger before you leave?" said R

"where is it?" said Ricardo

"second room on the right, it's right on top of the table" said R

so Ricardo went upstairs and went in the second room on the right. he got the charger but when we was going to go downstairs he heard a really quite

"ahhhhhhhhhhhhh"

he didn't know where it was coming from but he was curious. he turned to the opposite side of the stairs to look for where this sound was coming from. he then heard it again but this time louder "ahhhhhhhhhhhhh"

he then knew that it was coming from the next door. the door was open too, not fully opened but cracked open. so he then looked who was inside the room. when he placed his eye through the door's crack he saw that it was GB masturbating, she had her finger in her pussy going in a circular motion on her clitoris

he didn't go away and kept looking through the crack to see her masturbating, she was with her eyes closed so she didn't see him. then his dick started to get hard and when he noticed this and tried to cover his dick with his hand he dropped the sound box charger and that made a sound

"who's there?" said GB

Ricardo didn't say a word

"who's there?" said GB

"it's me, Ricardo" said Ricardo

"oh Ricardo, come in" said GB

so Ricardo got the sound box charger that was on the ground, opened the door and went in

"were you spying on me?" said GB completely naked

"i just heard something, i wanted to know what it was" said Ricardo

"well, now you know, did you like what you saw" said GB

"i did" said Ricardo

"so why are you there just staring, aren't you going to help me?" said GB

"i will" said Ricardo

so GB placed her hand on top of his dick and started playing with his dick on top of the shorts. when his dick was hard she pulle d it out his short and started sucking. Ricardo then took his shorts off and started to fuck her with her legs up his shoulder. he then pulled her legs down and hold them with his hands and started to fuck her like that. after some time he said

"i'm gonna cum"

but when he said that she placed her legs around his back in a way that he couldn't pull out, so he cummed inside her

"don't worry, i'm on the pill, i just needed to be filled with cum" said GB

Ricardo didn't say anything, and then she continued

"but now you know that you are my big dicked gigolo"

Ricardo then went downstairs, handed the sound box charger to R and went to his hotel. while this happened the guys stayed at the pool talking "i think they should subsidize hotels and restaurants" said R

"but you say that because you have an hotel" said MV

"i do, but it makes sense" said R

"why does it make sense?" said D

"just think about, the more money in the hands of the hotels and restaurants, the more pleasant experiences occur to the tourists, which means more of this tourist telling their friends back home of how pleasant the experience they had in the country was and the times this tourist will return to the country, meaning that more tourists will come to the country and spend money there, hence equalling to a higher gdp in the country, meaning that higher money in the hands of hotels and restaurants means a higher gdp." said R

"that makes sense" said D

"yeah, they should pass a bill about that, subsidize the whole tourism sector" said R

"i think they should sing be careful cupid in spanish 'cuidado cupido yo corro perigo tiengo mucho miedo de mi enamorar, yo sei como suefres das noches que lloran pidiendo siempre a dios un amor fiel'" said MV

"they should sing that in spanish" said G

the music was playing on the back and we were having drinks under the night sky, all dark but the glow from the stars, infinite universes, infinite dimensions all linked by black holes, all in sink under one sound wave beating continuous on and on forever and what are we in a universe of infinite dimensions but love

it's a central sound sphere and like the sun that radiates heat, it radiates sound and love to the entities that when they receives this sound and love makes sound and love but how many sound spheres are there, are you feeling me, woooooaw

there are various little colorful balls bouncing and bouncing peooooww peeeeooowww peooowww

"i think all the girls should take testosterone, their body will be looking insane" said G

"imagine that, all the girls with insane bodies" said L

"imagine JP with testosterone it will be looking insane, AA too, her body will be looking so nice" said D

"they put lulu leggings and those boots from uggs, those with fur, they look so sexy on those" said MV

"i think they should lower taxes" said L

"what? what does this have to do with girls getting sexy with testosterone and putting some boots" said MV

"they have too" said L

"what? what the fuck" said MV

"they have too, by lowering taxes there will be more money in the hand of the people meaning that more of this money will be multiplied, so how does this work, let's say we have 1 dollar being spent on lets say, a banana. than this dollar will go to the hands of the guy that sold him a banana. so this one dollar is going to be used on paying someone wages right, then this dollar is already 2 dollars, because this one dollar was used once for the banana buying and once on the wage paying, but then this dollar that is already 2 dollars is then used to buy, lets say, an apple. then this dollar is already 3 dollars, because the same dollar have been used 3 times, so this is the theory of economic multiplication, so the more money that is on the pocket of the people the mor e money that is going to be spent and multiplied, so yes i also agree that we should lower taxes to stimulate the economy" said L

"i never thought this way" said MV

"it makes sense" said G

"but wouldn't that mean less money in the hand of the government?" said D

"but the economy would be stronger" said L

"i prefer more money in the use of building highways and infrastructure, but i gotta confess having more money sounds better" said G

"but with a stronger economy more jobs will be made since the investors and entrepreneurs would feel more confident to invest in a growing economy" said R

"fair point" said G

"do you guys prefer blondes or brunettes?" said R

"i prefer brunette" said G

"i don't know for me, maybe blondes" said L

"for me blondes too" said MV

"black hair for me" said D

"you guys look like a bunch of whoozies prefering one over the other" said R

"don't get me wrong, i would still fuck the others" said L

"me too, this is like if they two come at you then i would prefer this one" said MV

"but what if the other one is hotter" said R

"then the other one, but if they are equally hot then the brunette" said G

"blondes are nice, but for me the defining factors are the ass and the abs" said R

"that's true, they need to have a nice abs too" said MV

"and an ass" said R

"unless we are talking of those tall skinny models, because they sexy as hell but they don't have a big ass" R continued

"but they do have a nice ass" said L

"but its not like really big, just really nice" said R

"but they work out too, they just don't get a big ass because of the workout they do" said G

"probably they do a lot of cardio too" said D

"but they look nice as hell, especially when they are tall, a girl like 1,70, 1,75 look nice as hell when she put those high heels and she is by your stature" said R

"yeah, but I can't get one of those for me, it will be looking really bad with me" said G

"yeah, but you are small, you need a petite one" said R

"yeah, i do" said G

"D can get a tall one though, MV and L too, just you really" said R

"i'm pist that there isn't a surgery to grow" said G

"you could have taken growth hormone but you needed to take that when you are young" said D

"Messi did that, I should have done it too" said G

"Messi is really crazy, he took his girlfriend to live with him in europe when he was 13" said L

"but Messi is Messi" said R

"must be crazy though" said MV

"i think he is the only guy his girlfriend has kissed" said D

"my girl has to like açai bowls" said R

"yeah, mine too, imagine having to go have ice cream all the time" said L

"what's the problem with having ice cream all the time" said D

"well, it's not a problem, but açai is better" said R

"yeah, because if she prefer ice cream, than many times instead of having açai we will have ice cream" said L

"i like ice cream" said D

"me too, I like of coconut" said MV

"really? I prefer strawberry" said G

"strawberry is really good" said R

"açai or strawberry ice cream" said G

"strawberry ice cream, but just like now and then" said R

"do you guys like pistachio?" said L

"i love pistachio" said R

"pistachio is one of my favorites" said MV

"which ice cream flavor do you like D?" said G

"i like cupuaçu" said D

"that's exotic" said G

"i'm exotic" said D

"common, you know what you are" said G

"what?" said D

"penis lover" said G

"have you guys ever sucked a dick?" said MV

"what the fuck?" said R

"just asking, knowing doesn't hurt" said MV

"why you asking though, having second thoughts on all the sashimi you had already" said R

"that is something that is not ever going to happen" said MV

"G seems like the guy that after he has 3 kids he will get out of the closet and marry some dude" said R

"he does seem like the type" said D

"MV too" said R

"my dick to you" said MV

"i'm gonna get out of your closet where i was hiding after i fucked your wife" said G

"it's a small climb to the closet so i don't know you can reach that high with that height" said R

"i wish they had a height surgery" said G

"you could have taken growth hormone when you was little" said D "but i didn't and now i'm like really small and there is no surgery" said G

"hold from those things you do pull ups, you get taller" said MV

"do you really?" said G

"no, you retarded" said MV

"what are your three best players?" said L

"Ribery, Ronaldo and Kleberson" said G

"who's Kleberson?" said L

"the one that played for bahia" said G

"i got to agree with Ronaldo" said R

"mine is Ronaldo first, Ronaldinho second and Cristiano Ronaldo third" R continued

"really? Ronaldo in front of Ronaldinho?" said L

"i mean, two gols in Oliver Kahn, he first for me" said R

"i prefer Messi than Cristiano Ronaldo" said D

"he is better, has more ability, what Cristiano has is taught, what Messi has he is born with that" D continued

"but Cristiano won more" said G

"in a pick up game i would get Messi first" said D

"just don't say that in the streets of brasil" said L

"why?" said D

"you can't say that you want an argentinian" said L

"fair enough" said D

"what about yours?" said R

"i would put Antony third, Vinicius Jr. second and Neymar first" said D

"the three of them are dangerous" said L

"i gotta put Romario up there, he even became a senator later" said G

"is he a good senator?" said R

"i think he is, he is like the one that most shows up there" said G "at least he is doing his job and arguing about the points that need to be taken care and is not there stealing" said D

"they elected a clown once" said MV

"was he good?" said R

"apparently he shows up there alot too" said MV

"i hope Bolsonaro wins this election or else brasil is going to get fucked with the workers party in power" said R

"yeah he have too" said G

"was he a good president?" said L

"he is good for the economy and don't steals, but since he is the only right, this shouldn't even be an argument" said D

"if the workers party get in to power there will be famine in brasil" said R

"probably" said G

"caos will break in the whole country" said MV

"do you guys watch basketball?" said R

"i do sometimes" said MV

"do you know the players?" said R

"i know some" said MV

"do you know who is Lebron James?" said R

"Lebron of course i know" said MV

"i hope he wins another ring with the lakers so he can be in the discussion of who is better against Jordan" said R

"it's about getting championships" said D

"who got more?" said L

"i don't know, i think it is Jordan" said R

"did you know that he hadn't lost one final" said L

"imagine that, never losing a final" said R

"yeah, but Lebron got more finals, so he has more vice championships" said L

"but in the end of the day is about the title itself, you don't want to gloat for a vice championship" said MV "if i was a team that was vice champion in the libertadores i would gloat about that" said L

"imagine bahia winning a libertadores" said G

"now that the city group bought them they can sign better players" said MV

"they have to improve the youth academy too, have more players getting out from home" said R

"that is true" said D

"but they have to sign top players too" said MV

"they have too" said L

"do you guys smoke weed?" said R

"i don't" said L

"i've smoked once before" said MV

"i met this guy once that only smokes with matchsticks, i asked him why didn't he buy a lighter, so he is kinda of strong and he told me that when he smokes he breaks a few to show how strong he is" said G "how big is him?" said D

"pretty big" said G

"i think it should be legal" said R

"of course you do, you like to smoke it" said D

"and you dont" said R

"i do too, but this will take a long time to happen" said D

"i don't know man, a lot of states in the united states are already recreationalizing" said MV

"even new york" said L

"but that is true" said MV

"i know that it is true, i was there 3 weeks ago" said L

"not that" said MV

"what then" said L

"that they should legalize it, take the money that is going to drug dealers and have this money pay taxes" said MV "but don't this make you get crazy" said L

"depend of the person, but no one is forcing no one to use, everyone uses only if they want to" said MV

"but that is true, have the taxes of the sales and use them to pay for schools and security" said G

"hey D, what was that country in europe that we got our feet done with those fishes" said R

"the one that the fish get all around your feet and when you take your foot out it is looking marvelous?" said D

"exactly that one" said R

"i don't remember really, maybe it was viena" said D

"do you remember L?" said R

"maybe italy, but it could had been viena" said L

"those are nice, do you think they have that in miami?" said D

"maybe" said R

"G do you know a place that little fish eat your dead skin of your foot in miami" said D

"no, not really, but we should find one" said G

"we could open one if there isn't that many" said D

"always good to open new stuff" said G

"i was thinking here, how can you tell if someone is a prostitute or not" said MV

"why, what you thinking" said D

"no, just wondering really, like i wouldn't want to kiss a prostitute" said MV

"i thought you were gonna open a strip club with fish that eat dead meat" said D

"he would run us out of business" said G

"he would have" said D

"so, how do you know" said MV

"is this a joke?" said D

"no not really" said MV

"well you look at her and you know" said G

"what if she just looks like one but she isn't really" said MV

"just risk it man, if she is who cares" said G

"she might charge you later though" said D

"that's the only issue" said G

"you ask how much, and when she says you say that you are a man whore and you are 100 dollars more expensive" said R

"she can kill you though" said D

"i heard this story that once this prostitute fell in love with a client and then killed him because she was jealous" said MV

"that's crazy" said D

"it's true" said MV

"imagine going to the motel thinking you are going to cum and then suddenly you get killed" said D

"that must be a bummer" said G

"that's cruelty" said L

"what do you think about the economy" said MV

"i think that we are in the start of a golden age, it will be the roaring twenties all over again. so this economist, Ray Dalio, was saying that the economy works in two cycles the long term and the short term, the long term happens every 75-100 years and the short ones are usually 5-10 years" said R

"what's your point" said MV

"that the end of the last cycle was in the house bubble that lead to the economic depression, hence it already passed the time that the economy goes down and now the economy will go up" said R

"you are not making sense, you are saying going up and going down" said MV

"what i mean is that after hitting the top of the economic cycle, the cycle then goes down, meaning that it will fall until a certain point. when we reach this point it is an economic expansion until we reach the top point of the cycle again, then it will go down again then up then down again" said R "i get what you are saying" said MV

"we are just lucky to be born in the right time" said R

"thank god" said G

"however there is a twist, there are players in this game, like usa and china, we play the usa game, but china is trying to make us play their game, and if they get brasil, then the macro scenario of the globe is in danger since there will only be left, america and europe, since china is buying a big position in africa and they are in asia so that is that, hence america got to help brasil place a firm right wing government" said R

"what the fuck are you talking about" said MV

"i'm just saying i don't wanna live in a commy world and they gotta do something" said R

"i don't too" said MV

"they should close china borders and place an embargo on any country that trade with china" said G "i think that is called the trade war and Trump did that" said D

"the embargoes weren't high enough" said R

"they should have raised them" said L

"i hope china doesn't conquer the world" said G

"me too" said R

"i wouldn't go there really, i don't like chinese, i like japonese tho" said R

"i fucked a korean two days ago, woaw that was my first asian pussy" said MV

"you never fucked an asian before" said D

"no, they are tight" said MV

"i haven't fucked one" said D

"i wouldn't go to asia tho" said MV

"africa too, too dangerous" MV then said

"i would just go to united states and europe" MV continued

"i don't know, i would like to travel around the world to africa and asia too" said D

"too dangerous" said MV

"if you go to the tourist parts of the town you are fine" said D

"do you think the murderer will care" said MV

"they don't murder tourists because then the cops get then" said D

"but it could happen" said MV

"and you could suck a dick" said D

"i heard this billionaire one saying, that he wanted to put chips in our brains, but he also said that life is a simulation, but wouldn't that make a loop" said R

"maybe is a cheat code" said G

"by doing so you prolong your life" G continued

"how so?" said L

"because, you know" said G

"i know what motherfucker" said L

"so you put the chip in and it becomes this extension of your biological self, connecting to the all the other times you've put one on and its infinite" said G

"but that's just a bad version of the baby theory" said R

"what? what the fuck is going on?" said MV

"the baby theory, the concept where we are all placed in a mechanism once we are borned and there we stay forever until we die of old age, yet this mechanism prolongs our lifes so we live a almost infinite amount of lives but eventually you do indeed die" said R

"so that isn't the simulation theory" said G

"it kinda is, you are placed in a simulation machine when we are borned" said R

"that's crazy, it's one or the other" said G

"there is only one" said R

"so what you think that happens when people put the chip" said G

"i think it makes a loop and then you wake up in a farm with pomeranians puppies and there is this old woman that says 'you don't need no chip'" said R

"what do you think happens when we die" said G

"i don't know, we would go to heaven" said R

"what is heaven like for you?" said G

"you go with the woman of this life to private island and stay there for like a long time, then you come back and party, and then you live so it can determine how the next one is gonna be" said R

"what the fuck is wrong with you" said MV

"and what is life?" said G

"life is the collection of loves you had with different people and each life you fall in love with a different one and live that life with a different one, then all these loves is combined and becomes your love" said R "what the fuuuuuuck? what the fuuuuuuuck?" said MV

"could it be that we go to another mechanism, could it be that what he is doing this to help us" said G

"could it be that he is a super villain and is trying to sell people heads to china" said MV

"what? what the fuck" said G

"could he do that like engineer wise" said R

"nothing is impossible so technically, but maybe he doesn't have enough time to do this on this life, but who knows generations from now. that is something that people have to take precautions from" said MV

"what if we die alot in life and it just skips to the next scene like a movie" said L

"there's a theory of physics there that says that whatever you imagine is already real somewhere" said D

"imagine that" said R

"what did you just did was like what then, imagine of imagine" said L

"what i do know is that Exaltasamba shouldn't have broken up, little T and Pericles should have made singles outside the group but they should have stayed together making song as a group" said R

"what if after you die it starts this huge rpg game and then it alternates like one life, like living a normal life and one rpg game and the movies and books during life are the highlights of your rpg game"

"what would you do in the rpg game?" said G

"i would be this huge dark net arms dealer" said D

"what would your name be?" said G

"mr big dick. imagine that, my employees that get arrested would be like, do you know who i work for? and the guys would be like, who? and then my guys would be like mr big dick and they will be like 'nooooooo, mr big dick nooooooo'" said D

"what if everyone speaks their own tongues and we just hear translated" said R

"i think it would be like we hear the mixtures of your tongue and the person you are talking, and there would be mixtures of different groups of peoples, but you never actually hears the person tongue itself" said G

"if someone wrote a book about this, people would probably burn them at a bonfire, they would think he is a witch" said D

"if i wrote a book about this and they crucify me i would be harry po" said MV

"what does that even mean" said G

"like harry powder" said MV

"i bet you would with all that snowflakes you put in your nose" said G

"you would still die though, witches weaknesses is fire" said D

"i wouldn't, i would make my crucifixes chopped dicks of my enemies, nobody would mess with me" said MV

"by the way, that would be a really good movie, a world were mages make crucifixes out of chopped dicks and the other mages have to find the chopped dicks of the mage he is hunting" said D "imagine that one mage looking for dicks to kill this other dude" said G

"no one would ever die" said MV

"maybe thats why we are imortal" said R

"i swear thats the theory of everything" said MV

"it gotta be, its the one most sensible" said G

"we probably just won the game" said MV

"what's next?" said D

"russia gotta be mad as fuck right now" said MV

"vlad is a sore loser he will probably start a war or something" said G

"what we did here is like giving a guy a nutmeg and when he turns you give that backward nutmeg" said L

"in the end of the world cup" said D

"if this was a book they probably gonna give this chapter for the kids to read" said MV "if this was a book i hope they pay royalties for that" said R

"there are some rich motherfuckers out there, there is this one Jeff Bezos, my dad calls him Jeff Bezerros" said D

"what does that mean?" said G

"like Jeff cows, my dad thinks the only way for someone to be that rich is by having many cows" said D

"he probably has alot of cows" said MV

"he should have alot of cows" said R

"are you guys going to this carnaval?" said G

"i'm going" said D

"carnaval is nice too" said L

"it is pretty nice" said D

"but you have to go to camarote salvador" said R

"i remember as a kid, i used to go to the trio eletrico and kiss many girls" said G "everyone did that" said L

"one thing that we were talking at miami the other day was if you are a doctor, a lawyer or an engineer, college is just for fun like this disneyland for teens" said R

"yeah, i remember. MV wasn't there tho" said L

"so what would you do?" said MV

"i would learn alot of programming languages and get a job then open something, create jobs you know" said R

"just get a bunch of those programming language for dummies books and read them, its way cheaper and you can get high paying jobs without a diploma" said R

"i think Mark did this, he read one of those when he was 10" said L

"but Mark is not a parameter he was a bibi when he was 23" said MV

"did you see how buff he is right now?" said R

"Jeff Bezos too, they probably take testo" R continued

"that's what you on?" said G

"it is" said R

"just don't tell that to the guys that came up with the idea of facebook" said D

"fuck them man, this is a world for winners" said R

"that's true, how can they tell him his idea" said G

"they are billionaires now though, they made this huge move on bitcoin" said MV

"Jamie Dimon said that crypto is a bust, that it only work for financing the dark net" said R

"but then he bought some bitcoin" R continued

"if this was a simulation how would it be?" said L

"maybe what we just said" said D

"but like what?" said L

"so it could be like this, its this infinite love game where you have different loves and like you live different lifes so you have a bunch of wifes, so each wife has a dad right, so if something wrong happens to you then he goes and safe you because he can't have this one thing affect her baby, but if you have a bunch of wifes, then you have alot of fathers to protect you" said R

"what if it a player versus player situation" said L

"then the stronger one wins" said R

"what if one guys have one wife and this other one has a bunch" said L

"then the other fathers will get together against this one father" said R

"then if the fathers got together would they win" said L

"they could, but it could also be this experiment on what percentage of total richness someone has to be to beat a group of rich guys" said R

"wouldn't that be bad?" said L

"but it could be a security algoritmn designed to find how much money you have to put to resolve this one problem that affects your most fundamental piece of existence" said R "and what is that?" said L

"in this case your daughter, but it could be a son or a wife" said R

"it could also be a game where you go and marry the girl and get money from her" said D

"but that's what the girls do, what would they do" said R

"more naked pillow fights maybe" said G

"so when i dropped out of college my dad was like aren't you going to do something with your life, don't you have a gift or something, so i said my gift is to get women, he laughed and gave me a car" L then said

"if someone poor heard this they would be like 'they are just daddys boys'" said G

"so you say, dont you want to be rich, dont you want to your kids to be born rich from the work you've done, and they will be looking stupid and shit" said R

"what you think about abortion?" said G

"i think that is the decision of the parents" said R

"but you think it should be legal" said G

"i think that if either one of the parents want, then they have to have the child, but if both of them don't then they shouldn't have the kid" said R

"what if the woman doesn't want the children, isn't her body?" said G

"but the child is also from the man, she doesn't have the right to take the life of the man's son" said R

"this talk was trippy as hell men " said D

"i think i'm gonna go get ready for the party" said G

"me too" said L

as L said that, he got out from the pool and went upstairs to get ready. some of the guys stayed in the pool. he got to his room and entered the shower. he then went to his bag and got a blue beach short with white dolphins and red eyes, a white shirt and a black la hat. he then got downstairs and sitted down. then D got downstairs, he sitted down next to L. Then MV got down the stairs, then B, then C and M, then R, then JV, then silicone titted M, then J, then silicone titted asian A then BP, then GB, they got their atvs and then they went to the party

when they got inside the girls went to the bathroom, the guys as usual went get the tropical gins. they got their drinks and went back to the front of the bathroom to meet the girls. when the girls got out of the bathroom, they went get tropical gins. when they got back, we stayed a little on the back but in front of the stage. little T was early today, so he soon started. some of them took their sandals off and stayed barefoot feeling the sand on their foot, some went to the front of the stage, the guys switched their gins for some beers and went to the front of the stage. then when the show was done, they switched back to tropical gin and went back to where the girls where

"so your boyfriend gone really?" said MV to silicone titted asian A

"he is" said silicone titted asian A

"hmmmmm" said MV

"are you gonna fuck me later?" said silicone titted asian A

"if i don't find no one maybe" said MV

"i hope you don't" said silicone titted asian A

"we'll see" said MV

then silicone titted M turned to G and said

"which of my girlfriends you gonna cheat on tonight?"

G took a sip of his tropical gin, looked around and said

"with that question, i think it might be you"

she was like

"i can't, you got my friend two days ago"

B then got to D side and said

"i found a guy that sells drugs"

"nice, tomorrow we buy" said D

MV then met this one girl and then silicone titted asian A was just looking to see if she would be feed cock later tonight by MV. but then MV just kissed the girl and then got back to where the group were. silicone titted asian A was happy to see that. they weren't talking but they were close one from the other

the party went on until it was bright, but today it didn't had funk in the morning, only house music. i think it was better that way, i really like the feel of house music with the bright sky of the morning. VC was tomorrow too, so it would be a nice day, i hope he does a long set, those are really nice. but then when the party was done, they got their atvs and went to the village caffé and had breakfast there. then when they were done they went to the house and then slept, some of them at least.

day 4

The first to wake was silicone titted asian A, she got down the stairs on her pijamas drank a cup of water and stayed there. then some more of the girls woke up and went downstairs to get a cup of water too.

"hey BP what was the name of that guy?" said C

"Enzo, i think your was Eduardo" said BP

"not those guys, the one that you got yesterday" said C

"Frederico" said BP

"really good looking he is" said C

"did you see his friends?" said silicone titted asian A

"that's why i'm saying, really hot too" said C

"maybe today they are going to be there" said silicone titted asian A

"they will, i'll introduce you" said BP

"today is VC right?" said silicone titted M

"it is" said JV

"nice" said silicone titted M

"today is the day that is going to be the fullest" said J

"today and new years" said BP

then after they talked for a bit, the guys got down the stairs all ready to go to the beach. it was late but they still could see the sunset on the beach

"we are going to the beach" said G

"we will change and go, will you guys wait for us" said silicone titted asian A

"will you girls take long?" said G

"no, we will gonna be fast" said silicone titted asian A

"okay then, we will wait" said G

they then went upstairs and changed from their pijamas. they all putted bikinis and a beach skirt and some of them putted hats and sunglasses, while some others putted just sunglasses. they got downstairs and everyone followed to the front lawn where the atvs where parked and went to the beach

"where are we going?" said silicone titted M

"macunacasa" said G

so they went to macunacasa and when they got a table. the first thing they did was order a round of coconut waters. the waiter then brought them their coconut waters, then they ordered some rose wine "two rose wine bottles please" said G

"i think i'm gonna order something too" said R

"what you want?" said G

"i'll have the shrimp risotto" said R

"that's a good call, i'm gonna order something too" said G

"i'll have the shrimp parmegiana, and bring some appetizers" G then continued

"which appetizers do you want?" said the waiter

"bring 4 of your best appetizers, pick the ones you like the most" said G

"i'll bring the oyster stuffed with mushroom, you will be dreaming about this" said the waiter

"i'll have the grilled octopus too" said JV

the waiter then brought them the rose wine and some of them had a glass. then the appetizers got to the table and they started eating. then the plates started coming and they had lunch. there had some hammocks and some tanning chairs so the group decided to change places. when they got there the sun was setting, the sky was a perfect tone of orange today. soon an old guy passed by us and said

"space brownies, do you guys want one?" said the brownie guy

"what are space brownies?" said L

"brownies with weed" said the brownie guy

"i'm good, do you guys want one?" said L

"are they good?" said D

"they are, you can't even taste the weed" said the brownie guy

"i'll have two then" said D

"i'll have two too" said R

the brownie guy handed D and R their brownies and moved on to the next table. R opened his brownie and ate, D too. the brownie was good

"do you feel anything?" said R

"no, do you" said D

"no" said R

a while later the brownie hitted them both

"damn, this good as hell" said R

"it is" said D

"why does this high is stronger?" said R

"it is processed by the liver, it gets 10 times stronger when it is by the liver" said D

"but you are not smoking, you are eating, so your lungs are not getting damaged" said R

"yeah, but i would still smoke from now and then" said D

"me too, but i think that you need to be eating edibles more and smoking less" said R

"but you can't eat edibles everyday" said D

"but you can't smoke everyday too" said R

"true, it gotta be now and then" said D

"i heard this guy once say that the right way to use weed is to use alot once and then stay a period without using, then use alot again" said R

"but you could also want just to chill, smoke one joint every night after you are done with the day" said D

"i'm just saying that i heard this guy once say" said R

"depends on the person really" said D

"you could also smoke a joint every night after the day is done and now and then take an edible" said R

"you could, you could" said D

"VC should play a remix of Legacy by Jerro & Tailor in Big Beach today" said G

"that is a good song" said R

"hey D, are you coming with me to buy drugs?" said B

"i'll go" said D

"who else wants?" said B

"what does he have?" said BP

"e" said B

"i'm good" said BP

"i'll have one" said R

"let's go then" said B

the sun was setting, it was already more dark than bright when we went get the atvs, we got on them and went to find the guy

"is this the house?" said D

"i think it is" said B

"look at the number" said D

"yeah, is this one" said B

we knocked, when the guy opened the door he said

"whhhhaaatttttt's upppppppppp"

"whaaats's uppppp mannnnnnn" said B

"come in, come in" said the guy

"how was your party last night?" said B

"really good, many girls, oh you are gay i forgot" said the guy "come here, come here" said the guy sitting down

"so, i just have 2 e and a gummy, i don't have 3 e" said the guy

"i'll take the e" said R

"i'll take the e" said B

"okay, i'll take the gummy" said D

"see you guys tonight" said the guy

then the three of them left. they got to the atvs and went to their house. they got there and went to the front pool table and sitted there waiting the rest of the people come back. then, a bit later, the guys and the girls started to come from the beach. most of them sitted down on the table and some them got drinks and started drinking

"what are you drinking?" said MV

"gin and red bull" said silicone titted M

"oh, i am gonna get one too" said MV

"get a cup for me" said R

"okay" said MV

he then went inside the kitchen and got two cups. he then returned to the pool front table and handed R his cup. he then poured himself a drink and then R did the same.

"i can't wait to see VC tonight" said JV

"i heard someone say yesterday that he will only come later tonight" said C

"but how late?" said JV

"probably like not until 4" said C

"today will be crazy" said JV

"i can't wait" said BP

"hey B did you get your party favors?" said silicone titted M

"i did" said B

"you gonna give me a bite" said silicone titted M

"bitch, you should had gotten yours" said B

"just a bite" said Silicone titted M

"okay, i'll give you a bite" said B

"did you all get e?" said C

"D got a gummy" said R

"weed or sweet?" said JV

"sweet" said D

"you'll be seeing things" said C

"i will" said D

"that shit is crazy, i took it this one time and got me all crazy" said C

"you look fine by me" said D

"yeah, but in the time" said C

"but its supposed to be like that" said D

"i know" said C

"i prefer e" said B

"me too" said R

"me too" said C

"well, it's getting late, im gonna go get ready" said B

"me too" said BP

then more people stood up and went upstairs to get ready. L was the firt downstairs, he was wearing a black shirt this time and a white shorts, he is thin so he looked good. BP and GB and J got downstairs too, they were wearing a white beach skirt and a top. then the other girls got downstairs. Just then D got downstairs wearing a white and black beach short and a white shirt. then MV wearing a red beach short and a dark blue shirt. then R wearing a small blue beach short and a long sleeves white linen shirt. they then placed their drinks on the table and went to the front lawn get the atvs. when they got to the party, they showed the silk wristband and then got inside. when they were inside the girls went to the bathroom. the guys went get a tropical gin. this time however, some of the girls went with the guys to get a drinks

"honestly, i'll have a vodka red bull today" said R

"that's a good call" said G

"i'll have that too" said MV

they got a vodka and red bull but D and J got a tropical gin and L got a gin and tonic. they then stayed there and a moment later the rest of the girls went to find them at the bar. they got their drinks, some tropical gins, some gin and tonics and then they went to the usual spot. a while later Little V and Skinny P got to the groups, they are old friends

"what's up" said Skinny P

"what's up" said D

"what day you guys got here?" said G

"i got here yesterday" said Skinny P

"you saw the waves here, there's a beach that has a righty really good" said Little V

"the beaches are nice here" said MV

"we were at macunacasa earlier, its a front beach restaurant, near the beach club" said L

"nice, we passed there earlier" said Skinny P

"nice place" said R

"really nice" said Little V

"you guys like VC?" said Skinny P

"i do, his sets are nice" said R

"what time does he starts" said G

"i heard it's like around 4 am" said Little V

"i think he plays for 4 hours today" said R

"maybe 5" said Skinny P

"maybe" said R

"i hope the sun is up when he is playing" R then said

"normally it is" said G

"remember that year, he was playing until 9 in the morning" said R

"really nice, we were in the front, really atmospheric" said G

then Little B which is this other guy got there. he is also gay. so him and B were talking

"hey Little B" said B

"hey B" said Little B

"i didn't see you the other days" said B

"i got here yesterday and i didn't come to the party, today is my first day" said Little B

"got here in the right day, VC is really good" said B

"i did, do you had time to buy any party favors?" said Little B

"i bought an e, do you wanna split it?" said B

"i do" said Little B

B then placed the e in his mouth. Little B then went there and got half of the e on his mouth. then when the e broke, B and Little B took a sip out of their drink

R also took his e and D took his gummy. it was dark outside and there had the lights of the stage, one hour had passed before this but then R turned to D and said

"do you feel anything?" said R

"i'm seing dragons" said D

"what about you" D then said

"i'm starting to feel it too" said R

then, G was talking to C and M too

"i don't know girls" said G

"what would you do?" said C

"if two friends wanted to kiss the same guy i think they both should kiss the same guy" said G

"then should we three kiss?" said M

they raised their shoulders and then gave a triple kiss. then C and M went and gave a kiss on each other, then C gave a slap on M, then C kissed M again

"wooooaw" said R

"what?" said D

"did you see that?" said R

"the slap?" said D

"yeah" said R

"i did" D then said

"what's up with them" said R

"love hate" said D

"they kissed again after" said R

"i saw" said D

then when G returned R, G and L meet this group of girls from rio, there had Sofia, Agatha and Antonella

"i saw you in the beach today" said R to Antonella

"i saw you too" said Antonella

"you guys look sexy there and here too" said R

"you too" said Antonella

after that G started to kiss Antonella, R kissed Sofia and L kissed Agatha. VC then started. the six of them where together and VC played, then the sun started to rise and when the sun was completely on top of them, VC was still playing. when it was 11 in the morning he stopped and then the six of them got out to the atvs. they had three atvs, so they got on them and went to the house and then they went upstairs. the six of them got inside a room and started taking their clothes off. First G was fucking Antonella, L was fucking Agatha and R was fucking Sofia. then they started to switch.

then Sofia went with R to his room and Agatha went to L's room, while Antonella stayed with G in his room

day 5

they woke up late on the day, but it was still bright out there. the girls from rio then said goodbye and went to her houses, the guys got a drink and got in the pool

"what would you do if a friend of yours fuck your girlfriend and sends you a picture of her saying naked saying that you need to break up because she is a slut and he fucked her yesterday?" said L

"probably thank him, why you asking, happened to you?" said G

"no, just wondering" said L

"i mean you can't get mad at the guy because he warned you" said R

"that's true" said G

"he still fucked your girl" said L

"but if he didn't then she would be fucking this other guys and you wouldn't know" said G "what can't happen is they stay together" said L

"true" said R

then D and MV got down to the pool. then, the girls joined them. they stayed there for a bit and after that they decided to go to the beach club. they got the atvs and went there. when they got there they showed their silk wristbands to get in and got a drink. then some went to the pool while some stayed outside the pool talking. some dj was playing.

"so you are moving to la" said silicone titted M

"i am" said MV

"yeah, it makes perfect sense" MV then said

"why does it makes sense?" said D

"because you can wear beach shorts during the day and a jacket at night" said MV

"that's good really" said silicone titted M

"yeah, new york is like cold cold in the day and cold cold in the night" said MV "new york is nice tho" said R

"but la is nice too" R then continued

"it is" said D

"but new york you can't wear shorts during the day during winter" said MV

"that's true" said D

"miami is nice too" said G

"but you cant wear a jacket during the night" said R

"why do you wanna wear a jacket at night" said D

"it looks good" said R

"it does" said D

"do you goes have tweeter?" said G

"i do, but i prefer instagram" said L

"why do you prefer instagram?" said MV

"i don't know, the girls can see you looking sexy" said L

"but can't you look sexy in tweeter?" said JV

"you can, but in instagram is better" said L

"i also prefer instagram" said JV

"but tweeter is a nice way to talk to people" said D

"but you have insta stories" said BP

"but you can't talk with them" said D

"but is nice to show what you are doing to your friends" said BP

"thats true, every time i go out i post a insta story" said D

"me too" said BP

"i mean, like not all the times" BP then continued

"yeah, me too" said D

"but twitter you can say your ideas" L then said

"you can" said D

"but like you can have both too" said silicone titted M

"you can, i do" said D

"but to share this moment of our lives with the people you care i think instagram is really good" said JV

"why you think so?" said R

"you can safe pictures of your best moments of your life as a recordation of all the moments and share it with the people you care" said JV

"that's true" said R

"imagine you are in this girl house and she leaves for a moment but her sister is there and she she starts seducing you, would you fuck her?" said G

"i would" said D

"you guys are dogs" said silicone titted M

"would you seduce me?" said G

"no, i love my sister" said silicone titted M

"am i dating her?" said L

"you kiss her from now and then" said G

"then yeah, but if the girl was my girlfriend, then no" said L

"imagine dating both at the same time" said G

"that would be crazy" said D

"would you date two at the same time?" said G

"i would" said D

"you have to be a real man" said G

"i am" said D

"me too" said L

"would you girls date someone with a friend?" said R

"i don't know, maybe" said JV

"would you date someone with a friend? said JV

"i'm not a gigolo" said R

"fair enough" said JV

"i can be your gigolo" said L

"would you really?" said JV

"i would" said L

"is there another friend we can make this?" said JV

"i was thinking me and you first" said L

"it could be too" said JV

"then i see you" said L

"see you too" said JV

when it got later they decided to go to the village have dinner before the party. they got there and they went to small ocean have dinner. they ordered some plates and juices. when they were done they went to the house. when everyone was done getting ready, they went to the front lawn to get the atvs. when they got to the party, they showed their silk wristbands and got inside, everyone was wearing white

a dj was playing and later on a funk dj would start playing

"i don't know if funk is the right move to spend new years" said R

"what would you have it play" said G

"house" said R

"i think that's the right move too" said MV

"what time does the dj starts playing" said R

"he probably starts later, not until 4 i think" said BP

"let's go get some drinks" said G

"let's go" said R

they got to the gin bar and ordered their drinks. first the girls. JV, C and M ordered a gin and tonic. silicone titted M and BP ordered a pink gin with tonic, silicone titted asian A and J ordered a vodka cranberry. then R and L got a vodka with tropical gin, D, MV and G ordered a vodka with regular red bull. they then went get some green grapes, you gotta eat seven for good luck.

the end

ps

"B we having a pijama party, do you wanna come?" silicone titted M texted B

"i'll go, what time?" B texted silicone titted M

"at 7" silicone titted M texted B

then when it was around 6 B got ready, putted his pijama on and went to the pijama party. he got there and they were drinking champagne and eating red velvet cupcakes. then it got late and they went to bed. a bit time later B heard something

"is it on" said BP

"i think it is" said GB

"let me check" said C

"it is on" then said C

"let's get this argan oil and put it on his dick" said JV

she got the bottle placed a bit on her hands and started to jerk B's dick. B then woke up "what? what the fuck?" said B

"have you girls tried it? i love how my mouth feels" said JV

"i don't think you should put it in your mouth, but using on the dick is really good" said silicone titted M

"untie me you dirty sluts, what the fuck is this?" said B

"i heard J telling me L did that with her, i only do it with that on now" said JV

"untie me, you girls are not gonna fuck me" said B

"girls it's not getting hard" said JV

"hold on a second, let me stick a finger on his ass" said silicone titted M

"you girls gonna stick a finger up my ass?" said B

"yeah, just turn" said silicone titted M

"you girls can stick the finger up my ass but my dick is not getting hard" said B

"we'll see" said JV

silicone titted M started fingering B's ass while JV sucked his dick. after a while JV stopped and said

"it's not getting hard"

"girl, you doing it wrong, let me try" said C

C started to suck his dick, then after a while she said

"it's not working"

"i told my dick is not getting hard" said B

"somebody stick a finger up his ass and i'll suck" said silicone titted M

she started to suck his cock while JV sticked a finger up his ass then his dick started to get hard, it got up and up until it was hard. silicone titted M then placed a bit more argan oil on his dick and started to sit.

"i knew you weren't gay" said BP

"i'm just bi" said B

"then don't say you are not trying to fuck us" said silicone titted M "i prefer man" said B

"so why are you fucking me" said silicone titted M

"you girls stuck a finger up my ass" said B

"it shouldn't have gotten hard" said C

"but it did" said B

the end

Made in the USA
Columbia, SC
18 October 2022